Reviews of The Book

'What an honour to be the first person to review this absolute gem of a collection of short stories and essays. I hope this book will receive many more... Recently I've been very disappointed with short stories as I've found them written in standard novel form only shorter whereas I've always thought of short stories as being a separate art form. The language should be more considered and measured, even poetic, to be able to invoke emotions and an affinity with either the thought, story or character central to the piece in a condensed way. Cresswell is a talented writer of short stories in their truest form. Her writing is elegant and profound. Each story captured a fragment of life in a moment of time and wrapped it within a satisfying tale. The stories shine a spotlight on individuals but highlights the human traits we all share.'

'It is not often you find a collection of short stories that are crafted gems such as these beautiful works are. Each tale is a carefully constructed entity that stands on its own, even those that are acknowledged to be taken from larger works. The book does what it should do, it gives pleasure and I sat and read it through without a thought of the time of day. The writing is thoughtful and studied but with such a light touch it was almost like holding a conversation with the author on a drowsy afternoon. A first class work that deserves to be read.'

'An absolute tour de force. The book should be prescribed reading for any course on short story writing. Each story shows that there is a very wise and observant mind at work – the essence of short stories – and each is beautifully well-constructed.

The writing itself is extremely powerful, and with its highly colourful characterisation and passages of description, the tales leave a firm imprint in your mind.

My favourites are from her time in America. Her descriptions of a fly-blown town in Texas and an open day in an old folks home are superb.

It's rare to be so impressed by the quality of a work coming from the Indie world, and I'm surprised that a writer of such calibre hasn't been picked up by the publishing world or awarded some prize. But I'm sure that this sort of quality won't be over-looked for long.'

Allie Cresswell was born in Stockport, UK and began writing fiction as soon as she could hold a pencil.

She did a BA in English Literature at Birmingham University and an MA at Queen Mary College, London.

She has been a print-buyer, a pub landlady, a book-keeper, run a B & B and a group of boutique holiday cottages. Nowadays Allie writes alongside teaching literature to lifelong learners.

She has two grown-up children, a granddaughter, two grandsons and two cockapoos. She is married to Tim and lives in Cumbria.

You can contact her via her website at www.allie-cresswell.com or find her on Facebook

The Book

By

Allie Cresswell

A collection of short stories, excerpts, reviews and travel journals

Contents

The Book

I can't remember, now, why I had to take the train that day.

It was late autumn, perhaps, or early winter. Very early morning, the pinkish promise of dawn only a smear above the rooftops. Cold. But the dawn frost didn't touch the grimy urban pavements. It only held itself as a crystalline possibility in the dry air, its glistening, hoary potential kept at bay by the damp, litter-strewn streets.

I was early, of course, having set off with contingent minutes for every likely and unlikely delay between home and the station. The platform wasn't empty, though. Others, like me, well ahead of time, (just in case), loitered like shadows in the twilight. They shuffled their feet and perused the listless noticeboard, reading adverts for events long passed that they had read the day before and the day before that. Some of them sipped from steaming Styrofoam, the vapour making halos in the barely-morning light. They were mainly dressed in city uniform; smart suits, warm woollen overcoats; grey, black, navy. Their faces, though washed, remained smudged with sleep. Their eyes were dull and reluctant. One girl began to apply make-up, smearing pale foundation over pale skin, enhancing, rather than diminishing, her ghostly morning pallor. Minutes passed. But the whole platform remained in a deep box of shadow cast by the ticket office and the waiting room of the opposite side, which interposed itself between us and the newly risen sun.

The idea of coffee attracted me, momentarily, but a glance over my shoulder to the Pumpkin coffee outlet showed me a queue five or six deep and that long-winded kind of coffee machine which dispenses the stuff drip-by-achingly-laborious-drip, and I dismissed the idea. I couldn't be bothered. That, then, was more or less my life's mantra: I couldn't be bothered. What was the point? When everything I had touched had turned to ashes and all that I had once dreamed of had proved itself to be no more than what had gone before; drudge and disappointment, dead-ends.

The tannoy crackled into life. 'Stand back from the platform edge,' we were instructed. 'The next train is a through train and will not stop here. Stand back from the platform edge.' Sure enough, the express tore through the station like a shrieking harridan, a pulsing blur of silver like a needle into atrophied flesh, with an after-rush which pushed us backwards and caused litter to dance and skitter. The hair of the girl doing her make-up whipped across her face and stuck to her tacky complexion. Mine, a hasty arrangement of random feathers and care-less curls, took momentary flight as though it might escape imprisonment, before settling back down to roost more or less in the same configuration. The vacuum of the train's wake sucked our breath from our bodies, but our expressions registered nothing, as though the train, or we ourselves, were spectres.

I walked almost to the end of the platform where a slither of sunlight had sliced past the buildings opposite to make a shard of brightness on the dull grey scene. A solitary girl perched on a bench, there, as though placed in a spotlight on a stage, and I gingerly took a seat at the opposite end. It was damp and cold, but clean. When I looked back down the platform to check the digital display I couldn't see it for the sun in my eyes. The others on the platform had disappeared into its shadow, their dark clothes and dull faces absorbed into the gloom. I checked my watch. Still twenty minutes to wait.

The girl on the bench was young, perhaps not quite twenty years old. She wore no make-up, had clear skin and almond-shaped eyes. I couldn't see her hair, it was completely covered by one of those brightly coloured, multi-patterned hats with a pointy apex and two plaited tassels suspended from ear-flaps. It suggested the Andes; Peru; a high plateau with brightly flapping prayer-flags and meandering goats; a hard, simple, happy life. Her coat was red, closely fitting with a nipped-in waist, a little grimy around the cuffs. Beneath the coat she wore jeans, and the bottoms of these were stuffed into warm sheepskin boots. The hands which protruded from the grubby cuffs held a book.

There was something about the girl. Of course she was unlike any of those semi-comatose commuters further down the platform. She was, like me, in the sunshine instead of, like them, in the shade. But she was, unlike me, illuminated in a way which had nothing to do with the wintery sun. She glowed with a radiance which seemed to come from an inner source, to light her up, almost to elevate her. She appeared hardly to be sitting on the bench at all, but to be floating just above it, so energised, so buoyed was her whole demeanour. Although she remained perfectly still on the seat it was as though she exuded waves of glee so palpable that they seemed physical. She was rapt; transported. Her face declared it. A smile played constantly around her lips and sometimes broke out, and the even teeth she pressed from time to time onto her bottom lip failed to subdue it one iota. Her eyes sparkled, they were wide with a kind of surprised awe, and full of laughter. I believed I could hear the occasional gasp or murmur of amazement but perhaps I conjectured these as the logical and irrepressible expression of her air.

She is meeting a new boyfriend, I thought, or has just left him after their first night of lovemaking. She is starting a new job, perhaps, although her clothes don't corroborate this. She is going travelling (again), back to Peru or off to somewhere else equally full of adventure. But where is her luggage?

I felt drawn to her, attracted by the powerful pull of her mein; intrigued, and envious of her youth and hopefulness and of this other non-specific but tangible current of secret gladness which emanated in appealing waves. At the same time I felt almost angry, resentful. Why, I wondered, should she have such evident cause for optimism, and I none at all?

In her hands she held a book and as the minutes passed by it seemed to me more and more apparent that the book was in some way the font of her happiness. Occasionally she would press her palm down on its cover, or trace its spine with her finger. I saw her draw her fingernail down the edges of the pages, almost as though it were an instrument she could play. Once she turned it over in her hands and I thought that she would open it, but she laid it back to rest on her lap. And all the while, she smiled, and projected gusts of private pleasure and knowing.

It was a hard-backed book of the old-fashioned type, bound in waxed linen of a brownish-copper colour. It looked, if not old then certainly not new; giving the impression of having been much-handled; not dog-eared or damaged, but definitely used. On its spine some tooling in gold lettering and an intricate perhaps quasi-Celtic design remained maddeningly unreadable as her hands caressed it. The front cover was blank, but from between the pages sprouted a number of different book-marks; ribbons, cards, plaited threads, denoting significant episodes or favourite passages. I have seen people with Bibles like this and, until recently, Filofaxes, their timely reminders and comforting reassurances marked for quick reference. But this was neither a bible nor a Filofax. It was a book.

The tannoy announced the next train - not mine, and, evidently, not the girl's either - and presently it arrived. I was aware of more passengers milling, the jostle of embarkation, but my attention now was so focussed on the girl and her book that I scarcely took any notice. Neither did she, but remained still, glowing and enraptured, and slowly caressing the book. Dimly, I heard the thud and echo of hurried footsteps and the growl of wheeled suitcases as they crossed the bridge from the other platform but they seemed distant and irrelevant. The station master blew his whistle and the train departed. It might as well have disappeared. My curiosity mounted with every moment that passed and took on a life of its own. The girl and her book felt like the whole world, like the only thing that mattered or would ever matter. I *had* to know, I *had* to understand.

'The next train on platform two will be the London train,' said the station master. 'Platform two for the non-stop service to London.'

It was my train. A fizz and rattle on the rails proclaimed its approach. 'That looks interesting,' I blurted out desperately, nodding at the book.

The girl turned wonderingly towards me, as though noticing me for the first time. 'Oh! Yes!' she said, giving me a brilliant smile which gathered up as into a bouquet all the effervescence, the simmering joy and astonishment which had budded and bloomed and perfumed the air around her for the past twenty minutes.

'What is it?' I pressed.

She turned it in her hands again. The wording on the spine eluded me once more. The train drew into the station and its doors opened. People began to press into the carriages. Others struggled off, shrugging into their coats, dragging cumbersome luggage.

I got up. I had to go. But some needy connection prevented me from walking away. 'Is this your train?' I asked, with a forlorn hope that I might persuade her to sit next to me on the journey.

She shook her head.

I was desperate. The platform had all-but cleared. A porter began to load parcels into the freight carriage. 'What *is* it?' I asked again. 'A holy book? A diary?' Down the platform, the station master consulted his watch and checked it by the station clock. A late-comer, a woman with a pushchair and a toddler in tow, burst out of the lift and he began to help her board.

She nodded. 'Both those. It's a life-story. Someone gave it to me earlier. Here you are.' Incredibly, she rose to her feet and handed me the book. 'It's yours,' she said.

At the last possible moment she stepped onto the train and the doors closed. The whistle blew and the train moved away, leaving me rooted to the platform, the book in my hand.

The morning rush was over. I could hear the station master and the porter making tea in their office. The platform was deserted, I alone remained, gasping and blinking, in the morning sun.

Tentatively, my train, my journey and everything else completely forgotten, I examined the book. The gold tooling on the spine turned out to be runes and curlicues of a language unknown to me; Russian, perhaps, or an ancient Aztec Sanskrit? I could not tell. I traced them with my finger, as I had seen the girl do earlier, and examined the fluttering ends of the ribbons and woven threads of the bookmarks which denoted episodes of special significance in this sacred life-story which had in some inexplicable way now become mine. What travels, I marvelled, what adventures and experiences, what successes, to have filled this volume and to have filled *her* with such a tangible vibe! My envy came back to me like a bitter gout of vomit in the back of my throat. What a paltry offering, I thought, what a limp and lifeless pamphlet would mine make, in comparison!

I opened the book and turned the pages.

Every one, from first to last, was entirely blank.

The shock threw me backwards onto the bench with the force of an express hurtling past. Realisation filled me up; water pouring into an empty vessel. Understanding frothed and fizzed and dazzled. The pristine whiteness of the vellum was almost blinding. It shone like a canvas stretched and primed and ready for paint; its glorious potential vast and incalculable. My fingertips tingled as I stroked the guiltless pages as though tracing Braille. The yet-to-be-written story ahead of me - a prospect so golden, so rich with opportunity and full of promise - beckoned and enticed.

Minutes - perhaps hours - passed in a sort of dream. Trains came and went again. People roamed the platform. I sat entranced and listened to the book's story of endless possibility, and thrilled at the high-points prophesied by those momentous markers, until I knew it all by heart.

'That looks interesting,' said a man I had not noticed before, from his seat on the opposite end of the bench. 'What is it?'

The Lake

Excerpted and adapted from a travel journal made during a stay in Michigan.

During October and November 2007 I found myself very unexpectedly in the US; but then, 2007 was a year full of surprises.

I stayed at a Hampton Inn - a chain of hotels very prolific in America - in Stevensville, Michigan. This northerly state is rather rural in character, full of orchards, dominated by the Great Lakes and its myriad inland waterways, but I didn't get to see much of it. I arrived in the small hours (without my luggage, which had given me the slip somewhere between Pittsburgh and South Bend) after a long, multi-legged journey which had started, in truth, only twenty four hours before but which felt to have been destined for twenty four years.

The hotel was pleasant enough, thankfully - it was to constitute almost my whole universe for the next six weeks. The room was a reasonable size, with a desk and an easy chair and a very large bed. Indeterminate artworks hung on the walls; blurry, as though painted by a myopic, indistinct blocks and hazy swathes of vivid colour; I was to spend many hours in their contemplation. There was a coffee-maker and a decent shower. Later, I was to discover the room replicated down to the last detail - even the art - in a dozen other states, but in the autumn of 2007 I was new at such things.

The window looked over the interstate - the roar of cars was constant, night and day; a howling backdrop to the heart of darkness I was to experience, but beyond that there were trees - a hopeful horizon - and during the course of my stay their leaves changed from green to red, then gold to brown and eventually fell, leaving stark grey branches against the rain-washed sky.

For the first few days I holed up - the only way I can describe my anxious, gone-to-ground existence in that bland cell. While my suitcase remained at large I was necessarily embarrassed as to attire in any case, washing smalls in the sink and drying them under the hair-drier, but the trauma of the trip, and the circumstances which had occasioned it, were taking their toll in a crippling backlash of self-recrimination and incapacitating timidity. I withdrew into what sanctuary the room offered, like a wounded animal, senses twitching on high-alert. The thunder of afternoon arrivals along the corridor, the rumble of their luggage across the harsh, commercial carpet, the heavy clunk of doors closing, left me clammy and palpitating with a sense of imminent threat.

What did I expect? That they would break in and harangue me? Drag me out by the hair for tar-and feathering? I don't know.

During the days the hotel was quiet, with only the whir of the lift (elevator), the occasional avalanche of ice in the machine and the drone of the chambermaid's vacuum cleaner to make a descant to the growl of traffic. I came to recognise the sound of her service cart as it wobbled its way along the corridor. My 'do not disturb' sign on the door firmly debarred her from broaching my defences. I watched her through the spy-hole in the door until she disappeared into the room opposite, then scurried out to stock up on coffee sachets and shampoo, cotton-buds, shower-caps - whatever I could grab - before scuttling back into my lair.

After a week or so, though, with the arrival of my suitcase and the world continuing to turn on its axle, I began to expand my horizons. I braved the breakfast buffet. The other guests - businessmen wolfing coffee and Danish, families gathered round the waffle-maker, Fay, the breakfast hostess - proved to be less daunting than I had feared. Whatever condemnatory labels I had pinned on myself seemed invisible to them. They ate and drank and created moraines of non-recyclable polystyrene litter, and ignored the woman wombling crackers and little tubs of

Philadelphia and pieces of fruit into her bag when she thought no-one was looking.

I started visiting the foyer where coffee was available and where the girls on Reception might engage in a moment or two of conversation. I began to look forward to these brief forays, a series of tiny exoduses; the lukewarm coffee, the 4pm cookie tray, the casual empty courtesies. They proved something.

I began to write, furiously, words pouring onto the screen with as much urgency as the cars hurling themselves down the motorway outside. A geyser of explanation and confession uncorked itself into lengthy emails to friends and family. I sent them off and hammered the send/receive hoping for replies. I read a little, when concentration allowed, and spent a lot of time staring out over the interstate at the trees beyond, pondering the seismic upheavals in my humdrum little life which had brought me to this pass; the devastated wasteland of ruined relationships and I had left behind me, the bright beacon which had caused me to do so, and trying to reconcile the two.

Day followed day and week followed week. The walls of my little cloister expanded to incorporate the entirety of the guest-accessible areas: the vending machines, the laundry, even the business centre. I got onto first name terms with the Receptionists, became intimate with the breakfast hostess and finally admitted the chambermaid to my inner sanctum.

I was ready for more. I wanted to go out.

It was an ordeal, a challenge I steeled myself to overcome but in the same way that the corridor, the stairwell and the breakfast room had ceased to hold any fear for me I felt sure that the outdoors could be conquered. I had no car - and, if I had had access to one, I doubt I would have had the guts to drive it. The hotel was miles from anywhere in the way that everything in the US is miles from everything else. From the entrance portico there was no obvious destination - no church spire or park gates, no inviting shop-fronts or friendly cafes where you could walk with apparent purpose - an errand, an enquiry, a valid excuse just to pop across... No. Just the soulless road endlessly travelled by car after car, flat, green verges, a fly-over and a vast expanse of featureless land of indeterminate usage; not residential, not commercial, not agricultural, not industrial. It was just *space;* rough turf and weedfields divided into plots, a perfect metaphorical wasteland. Going out into it was a step into the unknown, into strangeness and difference, quite terrifying, and, more than once, I baulked at it, and hurried back to the refuge of my room.

The outdoors - like life - offered me several directions, all hard and fraught with uncertainty, and, at last, I took one. I walked. I walked every day, doggedly, at first in the bright sunshine and then, when autumn descended, as it did, overnight, through gusty winds and drizzle. The first day I walked for an hour; half an hour 'there' and half an hour back, to see where it took me. The answer was: nowhere at all. No place that could be called a destination, nowhere that gave the exercise purpose. So I extended my range, walking for an hour before turning back, then for two, then for three. And I walked alone. In those weeks of walking, backwards and forwards along the same stretch of road, never arriving anywhere in particular but increasing my scope with each one, I never encountered a single other pedestrian.

It's a cliché, of course, but everything in America is BIG. The cars are big, the roads are big, the people are big. The pavements, however, are small; in some instances, non-existent. I walked, where available, on the grass verge, and, where not, in an area marked by a white line (no kerb) which I hoped was for walking on and wasn't some kind of hard shoulder, or, worse, filter lane.

At first I passed only amorphous plastic eateries selling fat and sugar and things sandwiched between slices of dough which would not have appealed even if I had had nerve to go inside. A CVS pharmacy was the most exciting and the only accessible shop I found for many days; much more than a pharmacy in the UK, it sold a wide range of goods and I trawled the shelves with minute attention. The CVS became a sort of basecamp to me, a safe-haven. I spent my first dollar there.

Beyond the CVS were other business I came to know well; they became markers, trig-points in my expanding universe. There is no ambiguity about American retail - they have a utilitarian, Ronseal approach which leaves no room for doubt; Coffee Express, Mexican Grill, The Liquor Locker, The Fireside Restaurant.

Presently the well-spaced commercial units petered out and residential estates took their place; they were all neat and pretty, but in some way vacant; I saw no children playing, no residents tending their gardens, no washing on lines. The names of the houses and lanes promised lake (Lake View, Lake Vista, Driftwood, Pine Lake Way) and one or two houses even had lake-going vessels parked alongside them, but not a glimmer of a lake could be discerned through the thickly vegetated gardens. I hoped for a sign: 'To the Lake' would have been good; the idea of sitting by open water was very appealing, after the confines of the hotel. There *were* signs, but they were not encouraging: 'Private', 'Keep Out', 'No entry'. Well, I wondered, gloomily; what did I expect?

Then, at last, on day three or four, I found it; an open, grassy space, a car park, and, down a steep scree of ragged cliff, the lake. It was enormous, like the sea, impossible to see the other side of it. It had waves like the sea, with white horses galloping atop, and a refreshing breeze blowing off which stirred my soul from the slough where it had slumbered too long. I found a grassy place beneath an old, scarred tree which clung close to the edge of the cliff and sat down on it. People in cars came and went on the tarmacked parking area, eating food from polystyrene boxes and drinking coffee from paper cups, and looked at the lake through their windscreens, insulated from the spray and the wind, sharp as a knife, which cut in from Canada. But I sat on the ground and breathed it all in.

Subsequent days saw me by the lake again. It drew me to itself with a kind of magnetism which made the resolute daily trudge past tacky fast food outlets and those shy, private houses seem like a kind of pilgrimage. The bewildering interior of CVS, the banter of the car-wash girls, the queue of cars at the window of CoffeeExpress were stations on the via dolorosa I forced myself to undertake each day. I don't know how far it was from the hotel - three miles? Four?

Michigan Lake is, to all intents and purposes, a sea. It looks like a sea; lustrous blue on bright, sunny days; silver like a mirror in intense sunshine; fantastical green on cloudy days or in the evening; turgid brown on dull, windy days; a bright, fiery red in the sunset - a blazing lake of fire. It behaves like the sea. Tidal, with waves which lap like teasing tongues in calm weather, but roil and thrash in the wind, ridden by white horses and the occasional, hardy surfer. It sounds like the sea; that eternal surge and suck and crash, with the cry of seagulls overhead and that peculiar and individual air-sound which echoes over vast expanses of water everywhere, searching fruitlessly for a destination. But it doesn't smell like the sea; that briny, ozone tang is missing, that mineral, vegetable, fishy sharpness which we breathe in on the seashore. And it doesn't taste like the sea. The water is fresh.

The beach, when you get to St Joseph's, which I did, eventually, is a broad swathe of beautiful clean sand, perforated by wooden palings designed to keep the sand on the beach as opposed to in St Joe's where it would undoubtedly drift if allowed free reign. Seaweed strews across it like the discarded clothing of an impulsive bather - or, more darkly, a suicide. It is bordered by a pleasant path – what we would call a promenade – with seats. These in themselves were a terrible rarity. I supposed if no one ever walked anywhere then no one ever needed to take a rest. But here there were benches, facing the lake, and some interesting modern street sculpture in silver metal which did not at all seem like an anomaly in the eye-searing brightness of the day I first visited. The day was warm and the wind, off the lake – there is always a wind – was pleasant and balmy. The lake was calm and sparkled like mercury. The occasional jogger or power-walker ploughed his way along the promenade. A little boy had fun chasing the seagulls across the sands. The peace was overwhelming; it seeped into me, little by little, a baptismal blessing, like the sand which infiltrated my clothes and hair and ears.

St Joseph's was a long walk - perhaps seven miles each way - but worth it. A proper little town, with shops, gardens, a café specialising in chocolate, an art gallery and a library. It was my rehabilitation, to browse in stores, to pass pleasantries with waitresses. I eavesdropped on couples in the gallery as they perused the exhibits, their ordinary observations were a kind of balm to my wounded psyche.

My most memorable experience of the Lake took place one evening, at sunset. The sky was on fire, red, the lake like brimstone, an inferno of elements. It seemed to leech all the colour from everything; gathering all peripheral pigmentation into itself; the woods, the dunes, the beach, me; everything else became grey and ghostly, translucent and ethereal. It took the breath away, drawing even that into itself. All the light and warmth, even mine, seemed concentrated in that molten place, water and sky. It was very beautiful, awesome, a vast crucible of everything; of life and continuance and the epic durability of the human spirit.

As I watched, it faded and shrank, and finally slipped away, leaving a dark vacuum within the hollow of the lake; silent trees and still water, a sky empty of stars. But I had the solid reassurance of a warm hand in mine, and I knew that I was real.

Very Kind Eyes

Chapter One of *Tiger in a Cage*

'Do you think you'll ever marry again?'

The question drops like a nuclear bomb into the unsuspecting peace of the fire-lit library. We are lounging on the saggy sofas, spread-eagled and spent by the rigours of the remote seaside holiday. We have hiked over tufted sand-dunes, and scrabbled along rocks treacherous with slimy seaweed, and shrieked as the tide chased us, and been buffeted all day by late autumn breezes as boisterous as ourselves. And then, arriving back at our temporary home, we have gorged on tea and toast, and now we roast by the roaring sea-logs which burn blue with salt. Someone has closed the curtains, but no-one has bothered to switch on the lamps, and so the library is mercifully gloomy, and in any case the glow of my face can be attributed to my position on the hearthrug beside the fire.

'Oh Lord!' I exclaim, perhaps a little too shrilly, 'I shouldn't think anyone will ever ask me!'

'Why not?'

I can feel the heavy, comfortable exhaustion in the room shift, fractionally. There is a draught of consciousness being drawn back from somnolence. Nobody moves, or, at least, I don't see that they do, but I sense the lifting of an eyebrow, the slight intake of breath which denotes that the interest of the others in the library has been engaged by my daughter's question. Or perhaps they are all asleep, and the draught I feel is only the lifting of my own shroud.

Somewhere in the inner reaches of the rambling, cliff-perched house, others of our party are beginning to emerge pinkly from early baths; the rattle of cutlery drawers denotes that they will begin the preparations for dinner. Presently there will be the plink and fizz of generous gin and tonics.

'Why not?' Lucy asks again.

I sigh, and stroke her hair back from her forehead; she is lying full stretch on the hearth rug and has her head in my lap. In answering her, I lower my voice: the reality is nothing to boast about; it's a hard reality, one I would rather not face, let alone voice, even to myself, much less in this room at this moment with its silently attentive listeners.

'Oh, you know. Once was something of a miracle, really, for someone like me. Who'd be interested in a plain old bird now?

'You're not old,' Lucy says, soothingly.

There is a muffled snort from the person who is lying on the sofa behind me, which could be a snore, but which eerily expresses my own inner indignation that she has chosen the age, and not the plainness, to deny. But in fact there is no point in denying either: I *am* old. At forty nine I am well past any prime I may fleetingly have enjoyed. My back aches and I have a map of thread veins on my inner thighs. My hair is going grey, something I do absolutely nothing to hide although I notice that I am unusual in this amongst women of my age. My figure is losing its delineations. This is something I do attempt to counteract, with a good diet and plenty of exercise, but feel increasingly that I am merely clinging on to the top of a slippery slope. I wake up with creases in my face which do not smooth away with the application of moisturiser, even the expensive ones which promise to restore seamlessness. Sometimes I sit in front of my mirror and with one hand on either side of my face, crease the flesh inwards towards my nose. The result is instant ageing and an appalling likeness to my mother. Oh God! 'This is what you will look like when you are seventy,' I say to myself, sternly. When I let go, the difference seems slight. 'This is what you look like now. Face it; your fantasies are girlish and ridiculous. Wake up, and smell the Steradent.'

'There must be *some* men who don't go for looks,' muses Lucy. It isn't a question, it's a thesis. She is pondering the idea. Oh! The naivety of the young! She is a strikingly beautiful young woman who has always attracted hordes of adoring swains and has already, at only twenty seven, had two quite serious proposals of marriage.

'Not many,' I comment. 'It's all to do with natural selection, you know - survival of the fittest. A man will be keener on procreation if he has a wife he fancies.' I hope, by this deliberately provocative gambit, to open the conversation up to include the others in the room, and to divert the subject of the discussion from my own personal prospects to the dynamics of relationships in general.

I fail. A slight movement of the sofa behind me suggests that its occupant has marginally changed his position; uncrossed his ankles, perhaps, or turned his head on the cushion, but whether that is in order to take more interest in the dialogue or to facilitate sleep I don't know. Julia, on the sofa opposite, has her eyes open and is staring with intensity into the fire. Her husband, Gerald, the fifth and final occupant of the room, fills an armchair next to the low table where our tea cups and crumby toast plates are stacked. He smiles vacantly at me and shifts his unlit pipe from one side of his mouth to the other. No-one speaks, and it occurs to me that my daughter's initial question was one which they had each asked themselves (and probably one another) about me in the past, and now they are simply waiting to have their curiosity satisfied. If that is the case, I wonder why none of them has come out and just asked. We have known each other well for years, thrown together as neighbours when we all moved into Combe Close and even after our enclave broke up, have continued to holiday, like this, on a regular basis. They knew my husband, and witnessed for themselves the less than happy relations which existed between us. Perhaps they are just curious to know whether my failure to make one marriage happy will make me less, or more likely to repeat the experiment. Perhaps this idle curiosity was just what had prompted my daughter's question, out of the blue. Perhaps I have no need to feel threatened. It is possible that I have not been rumbled at all. I am sure, as sure as I can be, that I have never betrayed myself by any conscious word or gesture. My tiger is safely in its cage.

'But just suppose…' Lucy says, sitting up and throwing another log onto the fire, '….just suppose that you did meet a man …….'

'A partially-sighted one, do you mean?' I interject, with an attempt at hilarity.

'If you insist.'

'And single, necessarily,' I add.

'I suppose so.'

'Of my own age?'

'Or older. Slightly older.'

'Well, there you are then,' I conclude, triumphantly. 'How many of those do you meet? You see, darling, the possibility gets more and more remote the more you think about it.'

Lucy gives me one of her looks, and throws herself back down onto the rug. Julia drags her eyes from the mesmerising flames and gives me a baleful smile. She evidently concurs with my conclusion. She heaves herself to her feet and announces her intention to go for a bath. Gerald makes no response and she leaves the room.

It is my belief that I have quashed the topic of conversation for good. It is particularly important to me to do so. To continue it in any kind of earnest might result in my revealing that in spite of the fact that I have no earthly expectation of marrying again I am utterly unable to quell the irrational and pathetically juvenile hope that love might come within my reach. Oh! I don't under-estimate the unfeasibility of it; my age, personal attractions and history of failure are decidedly against its likelihood, not to mention the strict conditions of integrity with which I am constitutionally prone to strangle its first tentative mews of life. Yet, there it is.

I am mistaken in my belief. 'So? Would you?'

'It's *so* unlikely,' I laugh, but there's an edge to my laughter which I recognise instantly as being the precursor to tears. The others recognise it too. Gerald sits up and begins to grope around the floor with his toe, searching for his slippers. Lucy gets up from the floor and takes possession of the vacated sofa. I assume that from my tone she detects that she has almost broken me and will soon have got at the truth, and chooses this elevated position to further pressurise me. I wonder at her cruelty; but then I remember her father. The man behind me makes the smallest noise with his tongue, like a tut, which I interpret, for the time being, as being impatience at my overly emotional response to a perfectly straight forward hypothetical question.

I grasp the nettle. 'Probably not, no.' I say. 'Even in the extremely unlikely event of anyone being prepared to overlook my age and unarguable hideousness, I would probably not marry him.' Marriage, indeed, makes no appearance on my horizon. But love, yes. Closeness, companionship, understanding – oh yes, all of those. I have, in the face of unattainable odds, pinned my hopes upon them, and the vision sustains me. I do not underestimate the impossibility of it, but then what evil spell of ugliness ever kept a prince from his princess? What enchanted forest of thorns ever separated a knight from his damsel? Doesn't love thrive on the impossible? Doesn't hope defy likelihood, and flutter its wings in the face of an onslaught of probability? Certainly mine has; though imprisoned in a tower of silence, it has refused to be reasoned out of existence.

'Humph.' Gerald says, suggesting that I have made a satisfactory answer. He gets up and stretches, then picks up the tray and carries it out. Evidently all my friends have felt it needed confirming that I had no matrimonial aspirations whatsoever. I wonder why this should be.

Charitably, I conclude that they all see how much happier I have been since Stan died; it's undeniable, I *have* been happier, in many ways. *They* have caused me happiness, through their friendship, but it is possible that they do not realise how important they are to me and just assume that I am unsuitable for the married state; that I am doomed both to make and to be made unhappy. Maybe they are better realists than I. They do not suspect the absurd aberration which is caged in the fortress of my matronly heart.

From the kitchen, I hear the jolly chatter of friends making dinner. The men joke and lever the tops off bottles of Schweppes, pretending to help with the cooking but getting in the way. The women clatter pans and gently scold the men, while the younger people are sent to set the table. In another room, someone is playing the piano, rather well. The noise from elsewhere seems to have relieved the intensity of the atmosphere in the room. It is as though a scene has ended in a play and we have found ourselves in the wings while the lights blaze on others posturing on the stage. The fire needs more fuel but we don't normally use this room after dinner and so we will allow it to die down. Later, we might play charades, or cards and there will be an elaborate effort made to ensure that I do not feel awkward about having no partner. These are my friends, and I have betrayed them all. My hope is not abstract; my vision no hazy anonymous fantasy. He has a name. He has a face. He is here.

Yes I have betrayed them, I think, but not more than they have betrayed me, with their secrets and private eccentricities that I have struggled, for twenty odd years, to contain. I have been the stopper on the bottle of the evil genie of their wayward impulses. It has cost me, though.

Lucy is lying on her stomach, now, reaching down with a languid arm and playing with the fringe on the bottom of the sofa. I really feel that I might have satisfied her curiosity this time and that she will leave the subject alone, but I am wrong again.

'Why not?'

I heave a testy sigh. 'Why would I not marry him?'

The man behind me is as still and silent as the sofa he is lying on. He must be fast asleep.

'Mmmm.' She doesn't look at me.

I cross the hearth rug and lean against the sofa where she rests her head, and lower my voice to a whisper. 'I wouldn't marry him just because he was available, or just because he asked,' I say, resolutely, 'I'm not *that* desperate. I know where *that* leads you.' I am speaking with a lock-and-key finality but before I can shut the door on it a gleam of light escapes from its prison, 'but if there was a man I loved, and if I was truly convinced that he loved me, and if we were free to be together without any...' shadows, I want to say, but I let the sentence trail away. Indeed I am appalled that I have said so much.

There is a sigh of breath long held but now released, like a dreamer moving from one dream to another. Simultaneously, my daughter says, 'Ahhh. You hope for that too, do you?'

'Of course! But I don't expect it. People my age have so much... baggage. Too many attachments. They're not free to make the choices that younger people can.'

We are silent for a while. Then she says, 'This man, what does he look like?'

Her penetration stupefies me. 'Looks!' I bluster, 'it doesn't matter what he looks like!'

'No, it doesn't matter, but what does he look like?'

I smile, nervously. This is becoming very risky. 'Oh,' I laugh, seeming to dismiss the question, 'he has a quirky smile, and very kind eyes,' I say, as if I am plucking irrelevancies from the air, like motes.

She nods, satisfied at last, and gets up from the sofa. Without a word, she leaves the room.

Slowly, I dare to raise my eyes to the man on the other sofa. He is not asleep. He has not been asleep. His eyes are wide open and they are looking at me, not for the first time, in a way which feeds my poor incarcerated hope.

He will not stay here in this room alone with me. I know he will not stay. That is one of the things I love about him; his goodness, his self-control; his and mine together form a bulwark which has kept us on the straight and narrow. He gets up from the sofa, but reluctantly. He walks to the door, then turns.

'You are not plain,' he says.

It only lasts a moment, and then the look is gone. Soon I will be left alone in a cold, dark room. But he looks at me before he goes, and smiles.

He has a quirky smile. And very kind eyes.

Many Rooms

St Quentin's square is somewhat off the main thoroughfare of the city's streets; traffic is admitted under sufferance and parking is not allowed. A quadrant of buildings and a narrow, peripheral, cobbled road hem in a small area of gardens. People like to use them at lunchtime and as respite from busy shops and workplaces. At midday the sun holds back the shadows thrown by the buildings; it is pleasant and feels oddly remote from the rest of the city. A pop-up café serves frothy drinks and cellophane-wrapped snacks. Sometimes, a busker plays. For many years now visitors have become accustomed to seeing three men in and around the square, as much a part of its architecture as the cenotaph which marks its centre, and as watchful.

The Commissionaire

Morning. The Commissionaire is the first to come. He materialises with the bluish dawn under the imposing portico of The Grand Hotel. Smart in a braided uniform, his inflexible decorum declares a military past. But years of comfortable living in his tiny apartment beneath the hotel eaves, and a regular supply of plated meals from the hotel kitchen, have broadened his girth; he is plump and rather florid, but his eyes are strangely sad.

He is an institution at The Grand, much-respected, although nobody, now, can remember why. The current staff is several iterations on from the one which watched the Commissionaire win his spurs.

He stands for the first few minutes breathing in the slightly sour city air and surveying the square with a veiled but proprietorial eye. The hardy gardens are really little more than a collection of very resilient shrubs and a determined tree or two. The plashing fountain is unfortunately a depository for litter and its bottom winks with copper pennies, the currency of abandoned hopes and despondent wishes which no one (so far) has been prepared to demean themselves by wading in to collect.

The steps of the war memorial bear poppy-wreaths throughout November. The rest of the year, people sit on the steps and eat sandwiches and lean against the names of the decomposed heroes. To the left of the hotel is the Crown Court; obdurate and magnificent. To the right, the crest-fallen church of St Quentin. Opposite are the bank HQ and the various barristers' chambers - an uneasy melding of old stone and plate glass.

The Commissionaire inspects it all solemnly from beneath the peak of his hat, until the first guest requires a taxi.

All day long he extracts guests from cabs and feeds them through the revolving doors of the Grand. He carries their parcels and fondles their pooches. He escorts them under the protection of his umbrella, keeping them dry while he, himself, gets wet.

At regular intervals his hand will travel discreetly to his jacket pocket, secreting five and ten pound notes. Those who proffer them do so almost as though they are not aware of it, as if their hand acts of its own volition, and he, equally, accepts with only a murmur; it is a vulgar transaction, beyond the dignity of both parties to acknowledge.

His expression is blandly impassive. Nothing from any guest will ever shock him; the Cabinet Minister who falls out of a taxi in fishnets, the ancient actress glutinous with implants and slap, the Oligarch's entourage - twelve strong, and all packing hardware - he greets them all with poker-faced deference. His conversation, if any, is restricted to mild observations about the weather, to which he will receive barely a reply, and expects none.

It is his job to serve without attracting notice. He is the impressive face of The Grand - designed to be forgotten the moment the opulent interior beyond the revolving door is glimpsed. And indeed he is forgotten, immediately, dismissed as a faceless flunkey. Beyond the request for a taxi or directions to the theatre, no meaningful remark is ever addressed to him, and very few people know his name.

The Vagrant

The man with the hat arrives in the square early, but not as early as the Commissionaire. By then the city is rousing itself. The street cleaner trundles across the cobbles collecting yesterday's litter. The Court janitor opens the massive doors and sweeps the steps. A handful of early office-workers scurry into the bank HQ and a very few would-be communicants loiter outside the church waiting for the priest to arrive.

The vagrant makes his way from whatever doss or hostel has housed him overnight and sits on the bench outside the Crown Court. If he has managed to get a bed at a refuge he will have had breakfast, but usually he has not. Hunger, like cold, penury, loneliness and ridicule, has become something to be endured; as mildly irritating as the wasps which proliferate in summer, and as impossible to overcome. He hunkers on the bench and takes what the day brings and in return, he offers the story on his hat.

The hat is formed from a sheet of brown cardboard formed into a cylinder and fixed into a brim. It is ridiculously tall and unstable; madder than the mad-hatter's. The entire surface is covered in words; the tiny, intricate penmanship is very fine, with flourish and curlicue, exceptional calligraphy executed without error by a master scribe.

He sits on his bench as the city stirs and stretches and comes to life; as Court business gets underway, as shoppers travel in by bus and tram, as traffic roars and growls outside the precincts of the square. Invariable, inevitable, day after day, the man sits on the bench with his bizarre hat perched on his head. The sight of him there in his peculiar hat is as familiar as the barristers in their gowns and wigs and the defendants in their unaccustomed suits. He's a fixture, a character, odd and faintly repugnant like the ever-present, oily pigeons. Like the cenotaph he is warmed by sun or washed by rain, whatever befalls, and remains in situ, seemingly impervious to either. Impervious except for his hat which darkens and droops in the wet, getting saggier and soggier until it collapses onto his head, its finely calligraphed story smudged beyond deciphering.

His hat is the thing by which he is known and of which he is most proud. If he catches a by-passer's eye one hand touches its brim, the other urgently beckons. 'Come and look,' he invites, with evangelical zeal. 'Come. Come and read my hat.' But the truth is that few people want to get close enough to decipher the words. They keep their eyes averted, fearing a tirade of senseless rhetoric or a long, sob-story outpouring from which they cannot get away. His hat and his evident destitution mark him out as a weirdo; unpredictable and possibly volatile. Their eyes skim across him as over an eyesore; politely myopic. His eager gestures go pointedly unnoticed.

In fact the man will neither importune nor harangue them. His hat is his story and is all he has to say. For a man who has nothing, it is all he has to give. For the rest, he enjoys a kind of famished peace; watching with a futile interest the comings and goings of the square.

The Priest

The priest comes last. Usually, indeed, he is late, arriving at breakneck speed on his decrepit old bicycle, his trouser-bottoms stuffed into his socks (odd, and often with holes). He hurries up the slippery, litter-strewn path to the church and unlocks the door. The meagre congregation straggles in, politely irate - they will be late for work. By the time he has scrambled into his robes and sloshed the communion wine into the chalice they will be half way through the Creed, having started the service without him.

Afterwards he watches them disappear into the morning crowds, leaning for a few minutes on the low damp wall which surrounds the church.

Across the square the man with the hat is already in position, pointing from time to time at his hat - newly constructed, by the look of it, after yesterday's deluge. The Commissionaire, very austere, brass-buttoned and braided, helps a lady with three pink poodles out of a limousine. The lady's hair is the same colour as the poodles'; it looks like candyfloss. The Commissionaire's face betrays no reaction whatsoever.

Behind the church wall are a few very ancient graves - so old that their inscriptions are lost. They teeter amongst the rank grass and rubbish. It is the priest's job to keep it tidy, a Verger being beyond the means of the straitened church, but he never seems to have the time. If he is lucky he will have time now to have a cup of instant coffee and a slice of bread in the arctic vestry, assuming the milk hasn't gone off or the bread turned mouldy, before pedalling off again at top speed in the direction of the hospital.

With a stipend inadequate to keeping body and soul together, he takes on additional ministry as Chaplain to two hospitals. He is also the Minister in residence at the crematorium. At every place he is a depository for the cares of the anxious, the ill, the lonely, the bereaved and the dying. They pour their tears into him as into a vessel and the salt is corrosive. They expect him to dispense wisdom and reassurance but he feels that his words are like pennies thrown into the fountain in the square. Their vats of grief are too vast and his expressions are empty gestures.

At the hospital an old woman is dying. She has nobody but the priest, who holds her unresisting hand while he mouths platitudes about the everlasting arms and the place prepared which he doubts can comfort, but her passing seems peaceful. Later he commits a body to the flames. His solemnly repeated promises of life everlasting sound hollow to his own ears but after the service the mourners press his hand and declare themselves comforted. By lunchtime he is back in church; an hour devoted to prayer and sermon preparation, but a parishioner wants to talk about his cut in benefits. He has a muddle of paperwork from Social Services and final demands from utility companies. Instead of prayer, the priest offers assistance, and they march off together to see the man's social worker leaving the priest's prayers unsaid and his evening sermon unprepared.

It doesn't matter. There is no congregation at the evening service. The priest recites The Owl and the Pussycat instead and goes outside to sit in the envelope of evening sunshine which slices obliquely between the court and the bank HQ to bathe the front of the church in brief artificial splendour. Despite the sunlight the priest's face is as haggard and in need of reinforcement as the façade of the church. The burdens he has collected during the day are like a teetering tower above him; he feels leeched of faith and drained of strength, his evening rounds of the wards and his usual vigil-hour at the hospital chapel way beyond his capacity. He wishes he could keep on sitting there, on the wall, while the sun goes down and night shrouds the deserted square. His soul cries out for rest and refreshment, but none comes, and the chiming clock above the court tells him he is late.

Serendipity

One January evening, the square is deserted. A heavy snow overnight and during the day kept most people at home and the city's commerce, like its traffic, has ground to a halt. St Quentin's square is slick with greyish slush, like gristle, its bumps and runnels indistinguishable from the granite cobbles. The fountain's waters are gelid, more solid than liquid, they rise up torpid and heavy, and fall back with a smack. The shrubs of the gardens are petrified and stark, the trees lifeless. The dusk arrived prematurely, hurrying the day towards night and now dank fog makes the air taste as wet and thick as an old cloth, so that breathing is like drowning.

The bank HQ and the chambers are unoccupied, the Court's doors firmly closed.

The hotel is empty. The chef and his commis, who live-in, are playing cards in the Porter's lodge behind the Reception desk. The restaurants are shut. The Porter will do duty at Reception if anybody comes. But nobody will.

The door of the church is ajar; a single, feeble light bulb glimmers in the porch and from within the strain of organ music sounds like somebody wailing.

The Priest is in the vestry, looking at donations for an imminent bazaar. There is no one else to sort through the dross and cast-offs which have been dumped at the church door, and time is short. The text for this evening's sermon was Jabberwocky; as good as anything, he thought, to a congregation of none, although, if the Archdeacon had decided to attend (which he has threatened he might) it would have given some cause for comment. Earlier, at the hospital, a tiny baby brought prematurely into the world had been taken as suddenly out of it. The Priest's shoulders are still damp from the tears of the teenage parents, as damp and threadbare and useless as the ragged trousers and frayed woollens in the bags piled all around him.

The Commissionaire, as always, stands to attention under the portico of the Grand Hotel. He shuffles his feet, discreetly, to keep the blood flowing, and plays out imaginary conversations in his head.

The man with the hat sits on his bench. He is cold. His hat is disintegrating in the damp air, its legend sliding, the ink seeping into the pulp, becoming blurred and irrelevant, like him.

Then: this.

The church door bursts open and the Priest erupts from inside. The sound of the wailing organ becomes indeed a human cry, wild and inconsolable. He runs across the cobbles and into the gardens, slipping on the wet slush, skidding to a halt in front of the obelisk of the cenotaph. His priestly robes are dishevelled, his face gaunt, his eyes bright and glittering with a disturbed light. The sound of his anguish ricochets off the blank facades of the buildings and comes back to him like the voice of another man in torment. His eyes cast around him, taking in the icy fountain, the desolate trees, the mute memorial, before settling on the man with the soggy, woebegone hat.

'I envy you,' he cries, angrily, stretching an accusing fist at the vagrant. 'Do you know that? I envy you!'

The man with the hat is so startled to be directly addressed that for a moment he does not respond. He turns slowly, left then right, to see who might be the recipient of the Priest's resentment, but there is no-one, and he lifts a disbelieving hand to point at himself.

'Me?'

'Yes, you.'

The man with the hat gets to his feet and negotiates the few steps which take him down from the Court's apron and onto the cobbles. The Priest comes to meet him. The Commissionaire, who has seen everything, finds himself descending the steps of The Grand and crossing the street.

'At least you have *time,*' the Priest exclaims, pointing an accusing finger at the vagrant, 'and nobody *bothers* you. You can *sit,* and *think,* and *pray!*' The Priest's face, formerly bloodless, is now hectic. He spits out his words, their liquescent venom melding into the foggy air and sprinking, a little, the front of the vagrant's grimy coat.

'Well,' the vagrant replies, hesitantly. Praying is not something he would wish to take credit for. The rest, he supposes, he can hardly deny. He reaches up to touch the brim of his hat, a reflex action; it is his lodestar, he knows where he is, with the hat. 'Well,' he says again.

'Now, now,' says the Commissionaire, calmly. 'I don't think we can blame...' he realises - they all realise - that the name of the vagrant is unknown, even after all these years. The vagrant himself finds he does not have it easily on the tip of his tongue. 'I don't think we can blame this gentleman,' the Commissionaire concludes, 'because we're run off our feet.'

'You're hardly run off yours,' the Priest replies, bitterly. But his tirade is over. He sinks onto a damp bench and puts his head in his hands. The vagrant and the Commissionaire sit on either side of him.

'Not today, no,' the Commissionaire admits.

'You get well fed, though,' the Vagrant says, rustily, 'and a warm bed at night, I bet.'

The Commissionaire nods. He can't deny it. 'But a machine could do my job. Come to that, people could get their own taxis and carry their own umbrellas. None of it *matters*. Nothing I do really matters to anybody.' The depths of his discontent surprises even him. The Priest and the vagrant turn, slowly, to look at him.

A thick shroud of mist billows across the square, blotting out the buildings. Somewhere in the abandoned city, a clock strikes the hour.

The Commissionaire, the Vagrant and the Priest

In the night the temperature drops so that when the sun rises the grey fog has been transformed into white frost. It coats the branches of the shrubs like sugar crystals and the surface of the war memorial winks and shimmers as though embedded overnight with crushed diamonds. The fountain is frozen; a petrified burble erupts from the centre of a smooth, translucent glaze. From its depths, a million pennies glint like granted wishes.

The Commissionaire steps out from under the hotel portico. His uniform is unaccountably loose on his diminished frame, but very smart, each button meticulously polished. The hotel barber has freshly-groomed the suddenly-overgrown hair, and shaved the oddly-weathered chin. Breakfast sits like a Christmas gift in his belly. When the first cab draws up at the kerb the alacrity of the Commissionaire's step to meet it is remarkable. Almost instinctively, he raises his hand to his hat as he escorts the guest up the steps. Its peak has been burnished to mirror-bright perfection.

The church doors are flung open wide, and music flows through them and out into the square. The Priest stands at the porch door, ruddy and smiling. His robes, through threadbare and rather tight around his girth, are beautifully laundered and ironed with military precision. He extends his hand eagerly to each congregant, engaging avidly with each, taking their burdens onto his willing shoulders. The Eucharist will be oddly disorganised but the worshippers are used to that; the Priest is such a busy man.

The vagrant comes to his bench ahead of his usual time, and takes his seat with a kind of diffident relief. He watches over the arrival of the workers with a benedictive eye, lingering on each one as they hurry past, his lips moving.

'Talking to himself now,' they tell themselves, 'he must be scattier than we thought.'

His hat is not so expertly constructed as formerly, and the lettering less elaborate, but more legible. The sharper-sighted amongst the passers-by make out the first line; 'In my Father's house are many rooms…'

Stoner

A review of John Williams' Novel

Stoner is in each of us, and each of us is in Stoner.

From the outside he is an ordinary, anonymous man; indistinguishable from thousands – millions – of others. He lives an unremarkable life and dies, and nobody remembers him, much.

And yet inside, *inside*, Stoner's life is a diorama, as ours is; a kaleidoscope of ever-shifting granules, some dull, some sharp, others iridescent. Within the little landscape of his life is a vista of hopes and dreams, a reality of drudge, moments of soaring passion and elevation of the soul, periods of disillusionment which is almost despair. Professionally, he has times of fulfilment, also sloughs of disenchantment. Often he takes the line of least resistance but sometimes he digs his heels in and refuses to budge. He has those occasional infinitesimal shifts of self-awareness and understanding which connect him for brief, glorious moments to himself, to others and to the world. But for the most part he exists in the semi-gloom of half-consciousness, extended periods of absent-mindedness and inattention which cause him to miss out on the mountain-peak moments which would have stayed with him to the grave and which, in the end, cause him to label his life as a failure.

Stoner's is a passive life – rarely is he proactive in his own fate - taking what comes at him with a stoic resignation; he is no hero, but he has a quiet honour. He makes wrong choices, living to regret the choices but embracing the consequences of them all the same, so that we can only admire the waste in spite of ourselves.

Am I not describing us all?

John Williams uses Stoner's ordinary, extra-ordinary life to explore the enormous gulfs which exist between what we see and what we understand, and between what we understand and our ability to express it. It is literature – a Shakespearian sonnet about death – which awakens Stoner from an almost insensate state to emotional life. Up to that point he is described in terms of the dead, dry earth; he is grey and brown, he is hard and calloused, he moves like an automaton feeding sheep and ploughing fields, he attends his classes and completes his assignments but his mind is not touched and his heart remains cold.

Then, an epiphany. The meaning of Shakespeare's words pierces his understanding; not just their literal meaning but their emotional, their spiritual significance. And he is completely, utterly unable to articulate a word of his revelation. Likewise in his marriage to Edith, the sudden drench of love he feels can find no expression in his mouth. The equally crushing realisation, when it comes, that his marriage is a failure, goes unexpressed and undiscussed. Only sometimes, in his classes, absorbed by his subject and almost released from the corporeality of himself, can what he sees, what he knows and what he says come together, leaving his students breathless and inspired.

Williams' depiction of the world is nuanced and multi-faceted. Often his descriptions are made up of juxtapositions; contradictory and confusing, but, then, isn't life? When is anything simply and only one thing? Any stone, when lifted and examined closely, will be found to be much more than plain unrelieved, unremarkable grey; it will have sparkle and colour and texture. And within – who knows what treasure, what mystery, what history it might contain?

Texas

Excerpted and adapted from a travel journal made during a stay in Texas.

How 'de from Booneville Texas where you join us in the middle of a plague of bugs.

We arrived yesterday from Philadelphia, a three hour flight followed by a three hour drive into the heart of darkness. As Dallas faded into a haze on the horizon behind us, the road unfolded beneath our wheels, grey and shimmering, dividing nothing from nothing - on either side, endless flat pastures, vast acreages of scrub unrelieved by topography of any kind. Clearly the early pioneers ran out of ways of describing this unrelievedly featureless landscape - we passed through a town called 'Pancake' and another called, simply, 'Flat.' In the fields herds of unpromising beef cattle kept company with dolefully nodding oil pumps. Strategically placed, every thirty miles or so, were billboards, enticing us onwards: Visit Sam's Bar, only 105 miles; Buc'cees – We Have Clean Rest Rooms; Eat with us * Get Gas (not a very appealing prospect for a Brit!) Surely, we reasoned, there would be something *civilised* at the end of our journey? The things we have got used to as symbolising civilisation here - Starbucks, MacDonalds, Dunkin Do'nuts, Applebees, TacoBell - were entirely absent, which should have been a relief - we find ourselves sickened, after a while, by the idea of coffee and snacks encased in dough - but, strangely, wasn't. Traffic, too, was sparse; often ours was the only vehicle in view, which, in a country where car is king, was a shock.

We travelled on into the afternoon. On the radio we could find only gospel or country-and- western, or evangelical preaching.

We did pass through the occasional settlement - town would be too generous a nomenclature although the Americans, of course, designate the smallest hamlet a 'city'. These villages got smaller and smaller and more like the sets of Western films; wooden clap-board, somehow insubstantial, you could imagine them being just flats, propped up behind, screening acre upon acre of nondescript scrub. They purported, however, to provide a shop or two, a town hall, a police station.

Every town has its church, and these (as in the north) are of a bewildering array of kinds and denominations: Church of Christ; Lutheran; Presbyterian; Methodist; Reformed; Anglican; Unitary; Evangelical; Baptist. And then there are the hybrids: Lutheran Methodist; Presbyterian Congregational; Anglican Evangelical; and the best one of all; The United Congregation of Anglican Reformed Lutheran Orthodoxy.

Without exception the church buildings are the best in town including the municipal buildings like schools and the post offices. They are splendidly well-kept, white and glowing, their lawns prick-neat and green, anomalous in the celery-coloured landscape, their dazzling spires reaching into the blue.

Houses are mainly trailers - semi-permanent, friable structures, leaning, peeling, with a wonky porch to the front and a dog tethered in the scrubby yard behind. They don't look attractive - in many cases they don't even look sound. One imagines rot and termites and everything covered in a bloom of gritty dust, unreliable plumbing, sporadic electricity. They are not placed in communities but spread out, miles and miles apart from each other, just plonked seemingly at random by the side of the road. The loneliness, day-to-day, must be crippling. Hence the enormous trucks almost invariably parked alongside - without transport, life, here, would be insupportable, although, one wonders, where on earth do they go in them? Trucks are more prized than houses, and more valuable, in many cases.

Hence also, I suppose, the churches. Without any other recreational activity less than fifty miles away, society centres on the church;

women's craft groups and men's bible-study fellowships, Sunday school, youth clubs, the Friday fish-fry, the Saturday night whist drive - these form the backbone of community life, a life-line in a wasteland of spartan fields and vast, empty sky. A good thing, you might say, and indeed, in the absence of anything else, I would have to suppose so. But also, perhaps, a slightly sinister aspect of life here in the hinterland; people are utterly dependent on the Church, they go because there is literally nothing else. For an enormous State - only Alaska is bigger - titanic and immeasurable in a way that we in the UK can hardly imagine - people in these remoter areas are very limited in their opportunities to experience first-hand other cultures or alternative points of view. What can balance the restrictive lasso of the fire-and-brimstone bible belt? There is a species of Christianity here which is as extreme and unpalatable as any radical branch of Islam you may encounter. Here, in Texas, some churches participated in burning the Koran.

This is not the America we are used to seeing on our television screens, but I think perhaps it is the real America. We have slipped over an invisible boundary, permeated the glossy image from positive to negative so that everything which seems advantageous about the US is now a terrible disadvantage; its vastness, for one. For space, freedom and rich resources read isolation, restriction and a hard-won living. There is a strong sense of the third world here, of a backwards civilisation, of poverty and hardship, dare I say it - of ignorance. What ameliorates life here is hard to see; no cinemas or museums, no shopping malls, no pleasant countryside, few trees. Where does a man takes his wife for a nice meal on their anniversary? How can young people meet and socialise? How soon, in an emergency, could an ambulance arrive? How would a gay person fare here? Or an atheist?

And so as dusk fell we arrived in Franklin, our destination, and what turned out to be home for the next four weeks.

Franklin is a sorry, dilapidated, desolate little town, arranged around a cross roads. A railway cuts through it. Trains sometimes a mile long - I have counted upwards of one hundred waggons - plough along the rails day and night, sounding their horns as they traverse the unmarked crossings. Franklin has a hotel - splendidly new, a Dollarmart (somewhere between a pound store, a Wilkinsons and a Superdrug, it sells everything from food to cheap nick-nacks), a Subway sandwich shop and a down-at-heel diner. And lots and lots of bugs.

As we arrived that evening, there were millions of them; on the pathways and in the grass, round the bushes; a leaping, boiling, crawling, rattling, whirring, flying, tentacle-waving mass. It was impossible to avoid driving over them, so thickly did they carpet the ground. Some were black and shiny with long elbowed legs behind and waving feelers at the front. Their wings were the shape and colour of mussel shells, they made a papery whirring noise when they flew and flung themselves against the windscreen. They lay on the ground looking dead until you stepped near them, when they leapt up with a whir of wings and bounced around in crazy unpredictable sallies making rattling noises.

Others were a brownish grey/green colour, larger than the black ones, with more legs and waving things at the front. Their legs were quite visibly serrated, presumably the source of the deafening noise which greeted us. They jumped much higher. I think they were in the middle of a sexual frenzy as there were a million small - presumably baby - ones of this kind and one great big one leaped repeatedly at the hotel door (which happened to be the same colour as him) trying to mate with it. Both kinds flew with all the aplomb of rookie spitfire pilots, dive bombing anything that moved with reckless inaccuracy, brushing past our faces with a nervous whir of wings. They were creatures of the night, filling the inky blackness with their scraping and sawing, chirruping and buzzing and yet fatally attracted to the light; the large lights over the petrol station were a mass of fluttering, flying things, dancing and swooping, gorging themselves on smaller insects also similarly drawn. The white walls of the hotel were covered with them.

As well as being a frenzied mass of life, they also represented a holocaust of death. They were mashed against the headlights of vehicles; they lay in drifts by the hotel doors exhausted by the effort of hurling themselves against the glass trying to get in. Those who did make it indoors died very quickly, either killed off by the air conditioning or trodden on by me.

Open Day

This is an excerpt from the first book in the Lost Boys quartet, Biscuits and Wee. Iris Fairlie has been placed at Bridge House, a home for the elderly, against her will. In the middle of an unusually hot summer, an Open Day is planned by the management and staff, but the night before, the weather breaks.

It pours in sheets all night long; a deluge of biblical proportions, and in the morning, although the worst of the downpour seems to be over, there is still a steady drenching drizzle. The lawn oozes with wetness, the gazebo and awnings flap and drip, and in the occasional gusts of wet wind fling sheets of water from their pooling roofs over everything adjacent. The seats of the folding chairs are all saturated and the ribbons of the May-pole have become impossibly tangled. The beautiful floral displays in the gardens are battered and flattened; water stands in pools on the baked ground. In the night one end of the Open Day banner must have become detached; now it droops dejectedly across a bed of ravaged roses. Mrs Terry, the Manageress, is besides herself, barking at the staff and residents alike, making hasty alternative plans for the Tombola and produce stalls. The nurses hurry everyone through the morning routine, and although Mrs Fairlie eyes the dresses with fiddly fastenings in her wardrobe she pulls on the trousers and jumper she knows she can manage herself rather than put anyone to any trouble.

On her slow walk through the ground floor and from her seat in the day room she can see that there is organised chaos. Stalls have been set up in the foyer and along the corridor, manned by relatives and cheery volunteers from the various church and women's organisations who regularly support the home. They are loaded down with jars of jam and pickle, cakes and pies and bottles of home-brewed wine. The tombola is crowded with a bizarre assortment of goods; toiletries and toys, plants and car accessories, a toilet brush, some crocheted place mats, an enormous stuffed Orang-utan, packets of sweets, satin-covered clothes hangers and sachets of pot-pourri. The Curate is selling raffle tickets from a small card table stationed by the entrance. There is a hubbub of conversation as stall-holders make the best of the new arrangements and bemoan the change in the weather. The carpet is dark with moisture from wet footprints and dripping umbrellas and the caretaker is trying to lay strips of clear plastic matting to protect the main thoroughfares, getting in everyone's way.

The school children tasked with dancing round the maypole have been corralled in the conservatory; it seems that the wet grass and driving rain will not deter them from exhibiting. They are shrill with excitement, squealing; their voices set the residents' dentures on edge. Outside their stout little teacher is struggling to untangle the ribbons from around the pole, her light suit growing quickly dark with damp across the shoulders and under the arms, her hair, specially permed for the occasion, looking frizzled. Everything outdoors is disconsolate, greyish brown and dejected. The bunting flaps like wet, psychedelic fish fillets from its string. The river has doubled in size, brown turgid water rushes past the banks now in a soupy flow. The Mallard keeps her ducklings close to her; they crouch on the grass away from the bank, the brown fluff of their feathers black and matted by the rain.

The residents sit around the walls of the day room blinking dazedly at one another. One complains querulously that she has not had her daily nap. A husband and wife cling together as though about to be riven asunder by some judgement of doom.

The ribbon has been strung across the day room; a good idea when the event was to be held in the gardens but somewhat mystifying now that it is spread around indoors, mainly before the ribbon can be arrived at. Mrs Terry wanted it moved to the foyer but somebody had suggested that the residents would, in that case, not be able to witness the ceremony.

'Damn the residents!' she had been heard to yell, but the ribbon remains in the day room.

The space is becoming more crowded as relatives and visitors assemble. There is an overpowering smell of damp wool and overheated bodies as more and more people cram into the downstairs rooms. There are dignitaries from various organisations, local business people, neighbours and well-wishers, relatives, of course, bringing with them children — 'just this once, it will make Granny's day' — sullen and under sufferance. Also present against their wills are prospective future residents, brought along under the guise of a pleasant afternoon out, but really as a subliminal introduction to the idea of residential care. They are not fooled. They scowl and find fault, thinking of their own arm chairs and their independence. A number of reporters and press photographers mingle with the rest. They greet each other with resigned smiles; 'Nothing doing here,' they agree in undertones, 'unless one of the old folks decides to croak.'

Before long the foyer and corridor is packed, with people spilling-over into the dining room and the small lounge; the sign declaring 'VIP Guests ONLY' has been knocked aside and is now underfoot. People are restive, wanting to begin the activities, eyeing the tombola stall and the produce, enquiring about teas. But the Mayoral party is late and Mrs Terry will not countenance a commencement until the protocol has been fully observed.

The unaccustomed noise and activity and disrupted routine are beginning to have a detrimental effect on the old people. The nurses disperse themselves around the patients, perching on the arms of their chairs or stationing themselves behind, stroking anxious hands and giving reassurance. There is an unmistakable and pungent aroma of urine in the day room. The nurses throw each other significant glances, but it is far too late to identify the culprit now and so the lavatorial lapse goes politely unmentioned.

Finally there is a rustle of excitement and the news permeates round the room that the Mayoral car has arrived. Mrs Terry is like a dog with two bones, quivering with self-importance and wagging her metaphorical tail. Even the school children are silenced at the prospect of the august arrival. The kitchen staff are ushered in, hastily tying fresh white aprons, and a waft of hot scones adds itself to the medley of scents already at large; wet clothes, hot-house flowers, distressed old people. The press take photographs of the arrival with eye-dazzling flash bulbs. Later, reviewing the press coverage, Mrs Terry will be dismayed to see that in every single picture her eyes are closed.

Mrs Fairlie finds herself placed next to Pinkie, a fellow-resident. Close to she is even more insubstantial; a mere gossamer of existence. Her skin is the finest translucent tissue over a tracery of blue veins and grey, bird-like bones. Her eyes, milky with cataracts, are sunk deeply into her fragile skull, the contours of her sockets as visible as smooth porcelain under their opaque membrane. Her hair is a diaphanous white wisp of down on the pink shell of her crown. Her hands are skeletal, claw-like, the twin twigs of her wrist bones disappearing into the sleeves of a candyfloss pink woollen cardigan which lies on her chair occupying the space where her body ought to be. The empty cardigan and some brushed cotton trousers in strawberry milk-shake pink, and a rose-pink cellular blanket take up the seat of a substantial wheeled reclining chair which can now be seen to house beneath it a discreet oxygen cylinder and a pouch of some clear fluid with a tube which disappears underneath Pinkie's clothes. It looks as though Pinkie's essence is being decanted into the pouch drip by drip.

Mrs Fairlie's attention is distracted by Mrs Terry's voice, yapping at the guests to step to one side and there is some good-humoured pushing and squashing as they make way for the party of dignitaries. Then the Mayor is in the room. He is a disappointingly diminutive man, dapper but thin to the point of emaciation; his heavy official chains seem to weigh him down almost beyond his endurance. Before cutting the ribbon he passes around the room stooping to greet one or two of the residents with a kindly word. Arriving at Pinkie's chair he reaches out and grasps her hand-bones with all the grim determination of a medical student commencing his first post-mortem. She smiles up at him sweetly, before asking, in a voice surprisingly loud and clear:

'And who the fuck are you?'

The Axbys of Top Farm

A fragment

Everything in Betty Axby's kitchen was exactly as it had been when her redoubtable mother-in-law had cooked in it, except that she had managed to persuade Jonas to buy an electric cooker for the summer months on the basis that it would be cheaper than leaving the Aga on all year round. Betty cherished that cooker; there wasn't a sprink on the enamel stove-top and the chrome of the hot-plates was as bright as the day it had been delivered. It was dated, now, its temperature measured in Fahrenheit instead of Celsius, and it had no fan, but it was hers – the only thing in the whole farm apart from her clothes that she could really claim sole ownership to. She still used her mother-in-law's old twin-tub although hefting the sheets from the wash to the rinse almost broke her back in two. The ancient old fridge, which still shuddered and jabbered in the corner, alternately icing up and leaking water from its perished rubber seals, dated from an even earlier generation of Axbys. The bed she and Jonas slept in had been his parents' beforehand and the antique bedroom suite likewise. The same square of threadbare carpet covered the kitchen flagstones. The original dresser displayed the Axby heirloom crockery. The single armchair which stood in the envelope of sunshine filtering through the narrow window was a pre-war survivor. In the evenings, Jonas took his ease there while Betty sat in one of the archaic sag-bottomed chairs at the table and squinted at the portable telly which perched on the end of the old sideboard.

Top Farm was the original Axby farm. Adam Axby, son of the original freeholder, was ninety now, and still lived at the farm. According to him it was still *his* farm; although Jonas and Betty ran it. They had brought old Adam's bed down to the front parlour three years ago, thinking his end was near, but he lingered still. All-but bed-ridden and stone deaf, he was still strong enough to crack the plaster with his stick on the dividing wall to get their attention and his notorious temper was still sufficiently incendiary to carry from his room, over the paddock, across the green and through the thick stone walls of the church where it appalled and embarrassed the handful of worshippers with its lurid and blasphemous connotations.

Jonas, the oldest of three boys, had inherited all of his father's cantankerous character. His voice could be heard as far as Chapel Farm on a still day – which was no accident - and his vocabulary was not choice. Poor Betty, a diminished, harried, perpetually aproned woman, was powerless to make herself heard between them. She cooked and cleaned and undertook old Adam's personal care, but whenever her thin, ineffectual voice tried to make itself heard, one or other of them would shout her down. 'You don't marry *an* Axby,' she had been heard to say, despairingly, 'you marry *the* Axbys. You throw yourself, your genes and your dreams into the Axby soup. And then they drown.'

Certainly, what dreams young Betty had had as she arrived at Top Farm as a bride had quickly been smothered by the weight of work both inside and out. Under the tutelage of her mother-in-law she had learnt to cater – it was an operation on too large a scale to be called cooking - for the vast and numerous Axby appetites. Jonas' brothers Amos and Eli had still lived at the farm in those days. By then Amos already had a wife and a steadily growing brood of children, stealing a march on Jonas which had really rankled. They all had voracious appetites which needed satisfying on the dot of eight, twelve and five. Supplementary sustenance, in the form of home-made cake and biscuits, was expected to accompany beverages between meals. Amos' wife, perpetually pregnant or nursing, had been excused domestic duties so it had been left to Betty and Mother Axby to produce three square meals a day plus auxiliary pastries, launder the family clothes and bedding and keep the house clean, as well as answering frequent calls to help on the farm in all weathers, calving, butchering the Christmas pig, keeping poultry, maintaining the kitchen garden and assisting the veterinary with vaccinations and castrations.

Jonas himself had not turned out to be the man she thought she had married. Tall and broad-chested with the distinguishing shock of white-blond hair and blue eyes which identified all the Axbys, he had epitomised the Scandinavian ancestry which the Axbys proudly claimed. All three boys had drawn her eye at the Breckersby dances but it had been Jonas who had crossed floor to ask her to dance and when he had taken her in his massive arms for the Viennese waltz she had almost fainted away. His courtship of her had had a brute animalism about it which had intoxicated and scared her in equal measure; he had punched a Dalethwaite man out cold for spilling his drink down her dress and carried her the two miles home when she'd sprained her ankle at a barn dance. When he kissed her she was left feeling limp and eviscerated. He took her to watch him compete at the Grasmere show, coming away with the gold medal for Cumbrian wrestling and her promise to be his bride. But once ensconced amongst his family his physicality revealed itself not, as she had hoped, as a demonstration of care and tenderness towards herself but only as a form of self-assertion; it was how he dominated and got his own way. In the bedroom his efforts were likewise a means to an end; he liked sex and took pleasure in having a wife, but essentially he wanted children, lots of children – like Amos, but preferably more.

Relations between Jonas and Amos had never been good. Natural rivals, they had spent their childhood and youth vying with each other for ascendancy, a noisy and bloody campaign which had not infrequently spilled out into the village street. But that was the Axbys all over; characteristically angry, opinionated and obstreperous; they could pick an argument in an empty room. Like their father both boys were over-large and over-loud, and over-handy with their fists. As young men Jonas and Amos could out-drink, out-shout, out-swear and out-fight any of their contemporaries but were only interested in out-doing each other. As they got older their father's early pride in their old-block attributes metamorphosed into a jealous defensiveness as he felt his own supremacy come increasingly under threat. He, too, would wade into the fray, taking indiscriminate sides with one lad or the other, often changing allegiance mid-stream in order to prove that he remained a match for them both. Between them all Mother Axby was not beyond adding her two-penn'orth, and a hard-handed slap into the bargain.

Eli, the youngest boy, had been of a different cast altogether; physically equal to his brothers but quieter and more contemplative. While undertaking quite his equal share of work on the farm and consuming quite his equal portion of the victuals, he had shied away from any involvement in the acrimony, letting it flow over and around him, or simply leaving the field of engagement altogether. He had become an instinctive if covert ally to Betty as she had striven to come to terms with the rancorous atmosphere of the household, the burden of work she was expected to undertake and, not least, the surprising speed with which Jonas had reverted to Axby type. Quietly withdrawing from the fray as the brothers harangued each other over the table or hurled insults from different rooms, Betty would frequently find Eli already ensconced in her chosen refuge; the hay-loft or the byre, or seated on the wall at the far end of the long paddock beneath the spreading arms of a magnificent copper beech, where you could look out past the church towards the sea. He would acknowledge her with a nod, and shift over to make room, and the two of them would sit in peace while the braying antagonism of the warring brothers, the booming interjections of their father and even Mother Axby's occasional incisive parries raged on.

Without saying a word Eli had somehow made Betty's life amongst the rampaging Axbys almost bearable; he would catch her eye as the brothers railed and Adam flailed and Mother harangued them all, and pass her the peas. On one occasion he came across her as she stood at the parlour window and watched, aghast, as the two brothers tussled in the mud of the yard in the pouring rain, and he had simply drawn the curtains and placed her in a fire-side chair. He stopped her feeling utterly alien. But then Mother Axby's sudden death put all the weight of the household onto Betty's shoulders and even if she wanted to escape to the hay-loft there was no opportunity as mouths had to be fed and the house kept clean. Moira, Amos' fecund wife, continued to produce one child after another while year passed year and no pregnancy ensued from Jonas' diligence. Without their mother's even-handed if acerbic intervention, relations between Jonas and Amos deteriorated further, goaded by Adam, until one evening one of Amos' children accidentally got pinned against the Aga during a scuffle, and something had to give.

The obvious solution was for Betty and Jonas to move down to Chapel Farm, a small satellite holding at the other end of the village with a recently rebuilt house and enough good grazing for a reasonable herd. Adam had bought it with a view to his retirement but without his late wife it had lost all its appeal. Jonas could certainly manage it if Eli went with him. It made sense for Amos to stay and help Adam at Top; the house was much bigger, for a start; there were four boys now and the three little lasses. The farm was more extensive and would support his clan; his oldest boys were ready to start helping out. Moira would have to stop having babies and start pulling her weight. Betty hesitantly intimated to Jonas that she would like the move; the idea of choosing her own furniture was appealing and perhaps if she didn't have to run round after the whole family there was still a chance that she might be able to make a start on their own. She had no objection to Eli coming with them – he was no trouble.

But Jonas dug his heels in. He was the eldest son and Top Farm was his due. He wasn't about to be palmed off with little more than a small-holding while Amos made off with the best farm in Tilting.

There followed a period of entrenched and vicious warfare. The brothers refused to co-operate on the farm so that jobs which needed two pairs of hand went undone unless Eli or Adam stepped in. The atmosphere in the farmhouse was caustic. Periods of stony silence were split asunder by sudden outbursts of vitriolic invective. Two of Amos' children started to wet the bed. Unprecedentedly, Moira lost a baby. The feud ground interminably on, night and day. Attempts at reasoned argument soon descended into pointless accusation and knee-jerk riposte and ended in smashed crockery and broken furniture. One evening the entire evening meal, product of Betty's labour, ended up on the floor. She fled to the hayloft and if Eli found her there and offered her comfort, who can blame her for taking the tenderness he offered?

Eventually Adam put a stop to it, sending Amos and his progeny off to Chapel Farm. Jonas, after all, was the eldest, as Adam had been, and Top Farm, was his birth right.

From that day on Jonas and Amos never exchanged a civil word. Betty became estranged from her sister-in-law and the clutch of nephews and nieces she had helped to nurture. Eli neither stayed at Top Farm nor went with Amos to Chapel; he left without a word. Betty missed his companionship in the hay-loft, his quiet peacefulness on the long paddock wall, and she sat there, sometimes, in the evenings when her work was done, and thought of him, and stroked her swelling stomach.

Baseball for Beginners

Excerpted from a travel journal made during a stay in Pennsylvania.

Yesterday we went to our first ballgame. We were taken to watch the Phillies play the Atlanta Braves. These games are played in series of three and the previous night the Phillies had beaten the Braves 7:0 so we expected great things for 'our' side.

The stadium is, of course, beautiful, with a magnificent view of the Philadelphia skyline; a sort of rotunda with food concessions all around the outside and then the bright green, immaculately mown field at the centre, with seats towering in layers right up to the sky. We were pretty high up but perfectly placed to see the scoreboard, without which I am afraid I would have been unable to follow much of what was going on. (My constant questions clearly began to annoy the neighbour to my right; the one to my left was almost as clueless as me.) The atmosphere is very jolly, lots of families having a great day out, all resplendent in red and white and enjoying the antics of the funny mascot down on the field and the roving fan-cam which energised them no-end when they found themselves on the huge screen.

Now baseball is a game of strategy and statistics, quite a lot like cricket; there seems to be a lot of hanging around and posturing and not much action. But instead of running up and down a corridor they run round a diamond-shaped square. But really they don't do that very often, if at all, so don't get too excited by the prospect of it or you'll only end up being disappointed.

The bowler is called the pitcher and he throws the ball at the batter who is called the striker – something of a misnomer, in my view, unless it is the kind of striker we associate with public transport workers, in which case it is much nearer the mark. The striker swung the bat around, balanced it on his hand, waggled it from side to side in a threatening, efficient-looking way, but of positive striking there was little evidence.

There are several types of ball the pitcher can throw (or pitch) which is not to say that the balls themselves are different but just that the type of throw varies. He can throw a ball which is called a ball, which means that in the view of the umpire it is not within the parameters required. (Surely, then, a 'no-ball'? Apparently not.) If he throws 4 of these balls the striker gets to walk to first base.

He can throw a ball which is called a strike, which does not at all mean that the striker strikes it but, on the contrary, that the striker does NOT strike it, even though he could have done, it being, in the umpire's view, strike-able. If the striker has not struck three strikes he is out, not out on strike, but out for the duration of an inning (also, it seems to me, an unnecessarily contradictory concept since an inning depends on three strikers being out, not in).

The pitcher can throw a ball which is a foul, because it strikes the striker. They pitch the ball at fairly impressive speeds – up to 95mph, so I guess the foul is so-called because of the language the striker utters when struck.

But none of these scenarios make an iota of difference to the score.

The score is only affected when the pitcher throws a ball which is a hit. I do understand that this is just exactly what he is NOT trying to do, and they are generally very good at it. It is, I think, the rarest occurrence of all, but essential for any progress to be made. Essentially a hit is a ball which is a strike (as determined by the umpire) and is also struck by the striker. Upon this happy serendipity of events the entire stadium is roused from its somnolence and rises to its feet in a frenzy of surprise and relief, scattering chips and peanut shells off their laps, spilling their beer and frightening small children, who have forgotten, in the foregoing doldrums of endless balls, strikes and fouls, walks and outs, that a ball game is happening at all.

So the pitcher throws a strike, the striker strikes it and it's a hit. Oh! Happy Day! It takes the striker a moment to come to terms with this rarest of phenomenon - there is an instant of palpable amazement - before he drops the bat and runs towards first base. But his excitement (and ours) is short-lived, either because the ball has travelled behind the striker and into the crowd (making it a foul, especially if it hits someone there) or because in that very brief space of time the ball has been caught without a bounce by a fielder (quite surprised to have anything to do) in which case the striker is out. Or, it has been caught after a bounce and returned with unerring swiftness to the first baseman who has caught it and arrived at first base before the striker, still overwhelmed by this unaccustomed turn of events, makes his bemused arrival.

Assuming neither of these scenarios, 'our man' on first must try to run or edge his way round the diamond as the next striker takes his turn. Sometimes we had as many as three men on bases, which would have meant three runs if the striker had only struck the strike beyond the reach of the fielders. But they never did. They struck it seemingly into the waiting gloves of the fielders and as a result everyone was out.

The score at the end was 4:1 to the Braves. Quite incredible to think that in the thee and a half hours we had watched, only five men had made it round the square, and none of them in very convincing style.

Now I am told that the skill of the pitcher is to make it very difficult for the striker to hit the ball. All well and good. But I must say that in my very inexperienced view it doesn't make for very interesting spectating. It is a bit like those tennis matches when players serve ace after ace and no actual tennis is played at all. I understand that it is incredibly skilful but it isn't very sporting. In terms of baseball it makes the whole game about the pitcher; the striker hardly gets a look-in, try as he might to meet the pace and curve and spin of the ball with his bat. The fielders are almost redundant unless there's a hit. A few good healthy thwacks of the ball while the striker raced round the diamond (this is called a home run, by the way) and the fielders scurrying to return the ball would have been much more exciting, made for a more dramatic score-line, more tension and better opportunities for crowd involvement.

It was a very warm day yesterday but rather windy. The gusts caught litter and winnowed it into unpleasant conglomerations of chips and ketchup cups and straws, napkins and greasy hot-dog papers around our ankles.

Grave Secrets

I live alongside the dead, but they don't bother me.

You might have seen my place - in the elbow of the sandstone wall which surrounds the burial ground. That wall keeps off the worst of the weather from the sea which pounds onto the shingle and tufted dune only yards beyond it. Even so, inside, the air is brackish and tastes of salt, and flowers quickly wither. Some of the older slabs are worn blank by wind, their memories erased; they stare out, vacant and vaguely troubled. At night my little lighted window shines in the blackness; constant against the restless wind and relentless waves and the shift and whisper of the unquiet ghosts.

It's my job to look after the place. I open the gates at sunrise and collect my barrow from behind the compost bins where shrivelled bouquets turn to ashy loam. I clip the hedges and keep the grass in trim. I weed the gravel in the garden of remembrance, and hoe the roses. They are obscenely abundant, blousy as barmaids - gorged on such high quality fertiliser - and their petals fall like outsized confetti, and their scent is like incense. In the autumn I collect the fruit from the memorial trees and leave it in boxes outside the gates, with an honesty box which usually gets taken, along with the fruit. They fruit prolifically, those trees. In fact everywhere you look - in the gardens and along the headstone ranks, standing easy, now, slant-shouldered, slouching, limp and lame, under the trees and through the shingles of the meandering pathways - life thrusts and pulses, clambers and claws its way out of death. Undefeated, in defiance, shoots push, buds swell, seeds explode, potent and exuberant, across the cemetery. As evening draws in I shoo out lusting couples and close the gates, and linger a while in the babies' arbour to comfort the bereft teddy bears and, last of all, before lying down, I relight the everlasting candle in the chapel.

Day in, day out, a constant parade of corteges passes along the narrow track towards the crematorium or to the place prepared for a final resting. They are not within my remit. The Crematorium has an administrator and a co-coordinator and a man who deals with the business end of things out back. The Council sends the digger for internments but these are rarer, nowadays. I put down my barrow and remove my hat for each sombre procession; my own greeting to the one in the lead, the one with the one-way ticket, who will not leave afterwards for sherry and sandwiches but remain here, with us, amongst the trimmed yew and weathered memorials. They'll be visited, of course. At first streams of tears and fresh flowers weekly will cover the raw earth mound or scatter-ground. Then - as the grass-seed sprouts - they will have ornamental plants, which last longer and need tending less often. Finally, artificial arrangements will decorate the grassy plots. They grow tatty and dishevelled but soothe the conscience for a grave unvisited. In the end all graves are the same; a forgotten patch of bare turf, a rash of daisies, with only the legend on the stone to tell one from another.

Mrs Toft, for example, one-time Alderman of the town, has a massive memorial, commensurate with her former position. Popular memory recalls her as firmly girdled with implacable jowls. A determined do-gooder and no sufferer of fools, she could hold a grudge much longer than her temper. Her stone is huge; square, black and hard as obsidian. It stands solid and impressive, mounted on a plinth and surrounded by railings in the centre of the cemetery with a small apron of grass in front where, in spring, crocuses and daffodils bloom. It seems like wherever you might stand in the graveyard, Mrs Toft's stone will draw the eye; larger, taller, more imposing than all the stones around. And wherever you walk, all the paths, however circuitous or meandering they may seem, will bring you face to face with it sooner or later. It is engraved at length (and huge public expense) with all her many accolades:

MARIA TOFT

BORN 1863

DEPARTED THIS LIFE 1938 AGED 75 YEARS

MUCH LAMENTED BY COLLEAGUES AND TOWNSPEOPLE

COUNCILLOR, ALDERMAN AND MAYOR

STALWART MEMBER OF NUMEROUS PUBLIC COMMITTEES, BOARDS
AND PANELS

BENEFACTOR OF CHARITIES

GOVERNOR OF SCHOOLS

OVERSEER OF HOSPITALS

A TIRELESS PUBLIC SERVANT, SHE SERVED THIS TOWN WITH
SELFLESS ENERGY

AND ROBUST DETERMINATION

'SHE LEFT NO STONE UNTURNED IN HER DRIVE TO DO GOOD'

At the base of the stone, on the plinth, smaller lettering declares the grave to be the resting place also of Jeremiah, who makes no claim for recognition other than as husband of the above. And in smaller calligraphy still, a circlet of lost babies chases round the entire memorial, half hidden by the nodding buttercups.

Jeremiah outlived Maria, but he is unusual in that. Almost invariably the men die first leaving wives who do not join them for many long years of weary widowhood. By the time some are reunited they have spent more years apart than they did together.

Look, here, beside the path.

SACRED TO THE MEMORY OF JOHN OBELISK

DIED 1902 AGED 44

AND TO HIS WIFE FREDA

WHO DEPARTED THIS LIFE IN 1961 AGED 98 YEARS

With what trepidation must she have approached her end and return to John, a stranger whose face she could hardly recall, a distant memory, a space where undying love has died away?

It is no surprise that at last the some-time lamented men are rarely joined by their wives, who have moved away, moved on, re-married, or for whom the prospect of being reunited would be just too strange a serendipity. These once beloved husbands are left to their solitude and singleness, each to his own plot: Colonel Abel Dovenby-Hall (Cold Stream Guards); Clive Broughton; Rev Brian Allonby.

It is perhaps to avoid this fate that sometimes the deceased decrees that the wife's name be added to the legend, ready for the time of her joining him below the sod.

Here's one beneath the yew:

HERE LIES MICHAEL PIMBLITT

BELOVED HUSBAND OF ELIZA

BORN JUNE 1852. DEPARTED THIS LIFE AUGUST 1913

AGED 61 YEARS

AND HIS WIFE, ELIZA

BORN OCTOBER 1860. DEPARTED THIS LIFE

AGED

Perhaps he meant it as a reassurance, that he would be there, waiting, a comfortable place prepared for Eliza when her time came. But there is a sort of insistence about it, isn't there? A kind of compulsion? It's an invitation which she declined. Whenever she departed, at whatever age, this stone does not record. Like Abel, Clive and Brian, Michael lies alone.

Not so the wives of Jonah Wardle; all five of them here in the wild corner, besides the railings; Mary, Susan, Bertha, another Mary and Joan. The ground here is rampant with acrimonious nettle, bramble, nightshade. The acrid wrangle of rank jealously erupts through the earth in vicious thorn, sting and bitter berry. No amount of weed-killer can keep it at bay. Of Jonah himself there is no mention; he declined to join the rancorous harem, choosing instead a peaceful spot at the top of the ground where the breeze is fresh and salt.

At dusk, when the gates are closed, and the sea beyond the dune is muted, shadows stretch across the graves, shadowed already by the silhouette of stones' long length, deepening shade to gloom and gloom to darkness. The trees whisper like hiding children. Somewhere within the burial ground foxes bark like solitary men with coughs, out taking a stroll. In that time of gloaming, sometimes, I can make out shapes; they move and flit and shift as light is leeched and darkness creeps. A flashing tangle of white petticoat is followed by a series of sharp slaps, as one Mrs Wardle lays about another, but might only be a bag caught on the railings. Mr Pimblitt mourns his wife's betrayal over by the yew, a long moan of recrimination as the wind sighs across the top of a vase. On the gravel pathway, where I left my ladders and a propped wigwam of tools, two figures stand stiffly side by side, exchanging no words; John and Freda Obelisk, whom even death did not part, unfortunately. And at the heart of the cemetery Maria Toft perches with dignity on the steps of her memorial, the dark stuff of her gown at one with the rich, black stone. Her husband Jeremiah hovers at a respectful distance, wary as an owl. The children chase each other round the little apron of lawn, and laugh, and glow, as the tiny solar lights begin to flicker into life, powered by the sun's borrowed rays.

On the Peach Side of Apricot (1)

Plain-Ann takes the seat next to the window. She is a neat, bird-like body of a woman, with bright eyes like jet beads. She wears a grey gabardine, all buttoned up, and a soft-brimmed hat against the winter rain. She gathers her shopping around her feet and settles herself for the journey as the bus lurches from the station.

Only Greta prefixes Ann's name with Plain, to differentiate her from Princess Anne and another Anne (scarcely less august, sharing the regal and all-important 'e') who presides over the Townswomen's Guild, both frequent points of reference in Greta's conversation. The jolt of the bus causes Greta to fall into the seat next to Plain-Ann; she had not been prepared for it. She had not been prepared for the rain, either, defying it to fall in spite of the weather forecast and the dark, threatening clouds which had boiled overhead as she had left the house. Plain-Ann's umbrella, commandeered earlier, has protected her jacket and stiffly-set, brassy hair-do but from the knee down her easy-iron trousers are soaked. She is a large woman, an imperious presence designed to dominate any proceedings. Her girth and an excessive number of shopping bags mean that she occupies more than just her section of the bus bench; she spills over into Plain-Ann's territory and onto Plain-Ann herself, distributing carriers and parcels as though the seat was vacant. It is always thus, on these bus trips back from town on Thursday mornings. Plain-Ann has decided it is better to be wedged in against the window than left perilously perched on the aisle-side where a sudden swerve could see her on her thrown onto the grimy, litter-strewn floor.

The two women are not friends. They live on the same road and catch the same buses to town and back on Thursdays, which is market day. Their daughters, however, had become friends at school, forging a connection which would not, otherwise, have existed. They have been coerced into co-ordinating lifts to Brownies and, later, cinemas and discos. Even though both the girls now live and work in distant counties, the Thursday bus trips are largely occupied with news of them, a subtly sparring, slightly competitive exchange of conversational one-upmanship, a rivalry not shared in any degree by the girls themselves, who have, more or less, lost touch.

Although the women travel together, they do not shop together. The first few moments of the journey are taken up with a desultory exchange of their mornings' doings; a cookery demonstration in the market hall, the scandalous rise in cost of the M & S café coffee and scone combo.

Then Greta introduces the topic on which, from the heights of her exhaustive experience, she is determined to pour all knowledge and sagacity. 'Tell me,' she says, like a priest inviting confession - there is nothing which can possibly surprise, shock or offend - but at the same time like an oracle, fore-knowing and pre-judging all that will ensue, 'where are you up to in the wedding arrangements? Invitations all in hand, are they?'

There is nothing that Greta cannot tell Plain-Ann about weddings; her own daughter Diana having been married, with great formality and style, the previous year. She can declaim - and has done so - with informed authority upon any aspect Plain-Ann may care to name - the venue, the menu, the role and function of the usher. She is thoroughly mistress of every wedding-related thing, necessity and nicety alike *ad infinitum*. And yet so far Plain-Ann has stubbornly refused to ask so much as an opinion. Her lips have been hermetically sealed. They remain sealed now.

'Yes thank you,' Plain-Ann nods, gazing out of the window.

Irritation overwhelms Greta. What's the matter with the woman? Surely everyone can benefit from a little advice? She decides on a prod. '*Home-made* aren't they?' she enquires, witheringly.

Her jibe finds its mark 'They're not 'home-made', they're 'hand-made',' Plain-Ann corrects her, sharply. 'There's a world of difference.'

Greta rummages in her bag for a tissue to cover her little smile of satisfaction. 'I stand corrected,' she says, tartly.

'Zoe came over at the weekend and we turned the dining room into a craft-centre. It was rather good fun. You'd be amazed how many processes are involved...' Plain-Ann's enthusiasm neutralises her annoyance. She speaks at some length, a sort of flood-gate having been, at last, opened up, although, up to this point, wild horses wouldn't have dragged the smallest detail out of her; she knows better than to bore other people rigid with arrangements for events in which they will have no participation.

 In celebrating this release, Greta is only dimly conscious of the detail, catching odd phrases, 'calligraphy ...lace trimming...origami... individually appliqued...'

'*We* had proper printed ones,' she puts in quickly when Plain-Ann stops to draw breath, eager to re-establish herself as the Fount of All Wisdom. 'Embossed, gilt-edged, with ribbon trimmings. I found a printer in...' and she is off, back on track, centre-stage.

Diana's wedding had been, probably, the happiest day of Greta's life. 'We only have one daughter,' she had told her husband, 'she shall have everything of the very best.'

There had followed a year of exhaustive researches, trips to out of the way suppliers of wedding favours, cut-throat negotiations with outfitters and photographers, florists and car-hire companies. Bridesmaids had been chosen, and screened, rigorously rehearsed, decked-out and meticulously accessorised. Ushers, likewise, had been drilled and bullied until able to fulfil their function with military efficiency. The wedding had absorbed all Greta's waking hours; her other interests - the Townswomen's Guild, the church flower rota, the whist club - had been sacrificed in its cause and all of this - every obstacle negotiated, every difficulty overcome - had been minutely related to Plain-Ann, week-by-week, as the bus trundled them to and from town.

The day itself had been a triumph of fluttering finery, opulent and flower-scented, the men top-hatted and grey-gloved, the women splendid, gorgeously outfitted in their very, very best and conscious of the honour they had been shown in being invited. Even Anne Barclay (President, Townswomen's Guild) had gone all-out for the occasion in a large-brimmed hat, her MBE proudly on display. The slow progress of the wedding limousines through the busy high street had brought commerce to a halt; every eye had turned upon them. Greta herself rigged like a galleon and escorted down the aisle by the best man had been only marginally outshone by the bride who followed seconds later. Afterwards, the peel of bells had reverberated across the vale to the farthest-flung farm.

'This is my moment,' she had whispered to her husband from the top table dais at the reception. Below them their guests were seated, strictly arranged as to due precedent, awed by wave upon wave of perfect gastronomy, overwhelmed by the class, by the style, by the expense.

Plain-Ann had not been invited. There had been no question of it. She and Greta were only passing acquaintances, after all, and their girls had lost touch.

Life, since Diana's wedding, has turned a little flat. News that poor, homely little Zoe is to tie the knot has reignited a spark. Perhaps Greta can, by a process of careful suggestion and judicious influence, manoeuvre herself into a prominent position in the limelight? Plain-Ann, after all - timid and retiring, socially inept as she is - will only benefit from Greta's hard-won experience. Without Greta to guide her she'll be overwhelmed before she even gets going, won't she?

But no. It seems not. Plain-Ann has her own ideas and has consistently resisted any friendly in-put from Greta. 'That's nice,' Plain-Ann interrupts now. The whereabouts of the printer is irrelevant, the whole topic of *Diana's* wedding of no possible moment. 'Zoe wanted something more *personal.*'

Greta puts the topic of invitations to one side. She casts about for an alternative outlet for her vast reservoir of experience. 'So the guest list is complete, then? Now there are a few pitfalls here; let me advise you, first of all, not to let the groom's people take too many liberties. Diana's mother-in-law claimed thirty seven first cousins, if you can believe it! I soon put a stop to that, as you can imagine. They were only stumping up 'a contribution' for the evening buffet so they had no room to dictate terms.'

Plain-Ann says 'I don't think that will be an issue, Chris hasn't much family.'

'And neither have you!' Greta says, as though acknowledging a delicate social failing. 'But don't be dismayed. Quality is much more important than quantity. *We* had an MBE, an MD and two JPs amongst *our* guests, not to mention a woman who had been at school with Princess Anne…'

'I got my outfit at the weekend,' Plain-Ann bursts out, sacrificially. Anything to ward off a roll-call of Greta's guest list.

'Ahh.' Greta nods, sagaciously. At last; here's a topic on which she can pronounce with authority. 'I hope you went to Debenhams. It's where I got mine. They had the best range, I found. Now if you *ask,* they have a private room with accessories that you can hire. Not everyone knows about it.'

'Thank you,' Plain-Ann shifts Greta's insulated Iceland carrier bag a fraction, away from her arthritic knee, 'but in fact, we went to a boutique which specialises in Mother of the Bride outfits. All their ensembles are on-offs. There'll be no possibility of any of the guests turning up in the same thing. They had a *huge* range of accessories, all co-ordinated, of course.'

Greta bridles, stymied again, but allows herself only to observe 'I hope they included coats. Take my advice and wear a coat for the church. I only had a jacket and I was perished, even in July. *I* wore…'

The bus pulls up at a stop and two ladies in traditional Indian dress climb aboard. Greta reprises her mother of the bride outfit in wearying detail.

'There'll be no need for a coat at all,' Plain-Ann says at last, in a quiet voice almost drowned out by the roar of the engine as the bus draws away from the kerb. 'Everything's happening at the hotel.'

Greta is aghast. 'Even the ceremony?'

Plain-Ann nods. 'Yes. They're licenced for wedding ceremonies.'

Greta's expectations undergo a seismic shift. So this isn't going to be a *proper* wedding at all! It is going to be modern, alternative, a no-frills, package-deal of an affair. No wonder Plain-Ann has been so tight-lipped. No church ceremony? Greta cannot prevent a sigh. What a disappointment! The wedding processional reduced to a quick scurry down a carpeted corridor, the lofty groins, quatrefoils and crocketted pinnacles of St Michael's replaced by the beige blandness of a hotel function room or, worse, the registry office at the town hall.

'I think it's much more *honest,*' Plain-Ann retorts. Greta's silence has been loud with disapproval. 'They have been living together for eighteen months. And neither of them are church-goers.'

'But what about the ph…'

'Diana said it would be hypocritical to have a church wedding just so that the photographs will look nice, and I agree with her.'

Greta swallows back any further comment. The bus descends a slip-way onto a dual carriageway; they will soon be home.

Diana's photographs certainly look splendid, against the backdrop of the church tower, a mullioned window, the bride and groom illuminated by a rainbow of light as it filters through the stained glass. Greta keeps the album on her coffee table, and shows it to guests when they call. But in point of fact the Vicar had been very awkward over the fact that Diana and Bruce weren't regular congregants.

'She's a member of this church,' Greta had insisted. 'You christened her yourself. Look! Here's the certificate!'

In the end, only a significant donation to the heating fund had swung it.

Then there had been all the difficulty over the hymns. 'Do we *have* to have songs about God?' Bruce had wanted to know. He'd wanted 'you'll never walk alone.' Diana had wanted to walk down the aisle to an Elton John song. Neither of them had been happy about the bible reading. 'We wanted that passage from Captain Corelli,' they'd said, 'and a Celtic blessing.'

Really, what with the reluctance of the Vicar, and the foot-dragging of the bride and groom, and the parsimony of her husband (*'two* lots of fees - the church *and* the Registry - *two* lots of flowers, *double* the distance for the limousines - where will it all end? Wouldn't a ladder and two tickets to Gretna have been better?') she had wondered, sometimes, if anyone really appreciated all her efforts? The weeks before the wedding had been embittered, the bride and groom raising objections over the least sugared almond, attending suit and frock fittings with extreme ill-grace, becoming sullen and unco-operative as though the wedding was an ordeal they were being forced to undergo, like the Vicar's prescribed marriage-preparation classes, rather than something they had chosen.

Last time Greta heard from Diana there had been the suggestion of a separation in the offing. 'All the stress of the big day,' she had moaned, 'Bruce and I have never really got over it. It's all taken its toll, Mum.'

Greta's husband is still working extra shifts, to pay off the credit cards.

Greta shifts her feet. They are as cold as ice, the damp from her trousers like corpses' hands clamped to her ankles. Next to her, Plain-Ann looks warm and dry; her gabardine might be drab, but it is efficient. The bus exits the dual carriageway and negotiates a roundabout. Not far now.

Perhaps, after all, Greta thinks, Plain-Ann's is a more sensible approach.

'What colour is it?' Greta asks, 'your outfit?'

Plain-Ann eyes her, narrowly. She knows that the mother of the groom should wear beige and keep her mouth shut. Is there, she wonders, some similar received wisdom for mothers of the bride which Greta is about to impart? She steels herself. 'Hard to say, orangey.'

Unusually, there seems to be no hidden agenda, no right-or-wrong answer to Greta's question. It appears that she is only interested.

'Like a tangerine?' Greta asks, conversationally.

In her surprise, Plain-Ann finds herself being more forth-coming. 'Oh no! Not so vivid. When I say orangey, really it's more orangey-pink.'

Greta lifts her Iceland bag off Plain-Ann's lap. It is heavier, and much colder than she had appreciated. 'Orange blossom, then? That'll be nice, for a spring wedding.'

'N.. no, not really. That's *really* pale, isn't it?'

'More of an apricot?' The bus slows and stops. The Indian ladies get off. Greta and Plain-Ann's stop is next.

'Mmm. But pinker.'

'Shrimp?' it is a deliberately facetious suggestion. They both laugh.

'No! Not as pink as that.'

They are gathering their parcels. The bus slows for a pedestrian.

'Coral, perhaps?'

'No. Not so bright.'

Greta reaches up and presses the button. At the front of the bus a bell alerts the driver. The woman sitting in front of them mutters 'Peach?'

Greta snatches it from the air. 'Peach?'

The bus begins to indicate and pulls into the kerb. Greta and Plain-Ann rise.

'On the peach side of apricot,' Plain-Ann concedes.

Greta nods. Behind her tightly-clamped lips a torrent of good advice seethes and jostles; the importance of contrast - in a scarf or the trimming of a hat - to set off the whole ensemble, the usefulness, on the day, of a capacious handbag, the absolute necessity of comfortable shoes. 'Sounds lovely,' is all she says.

They make their way towards the doors.

'See you next week, then?' Greta says as she descends.

'See you next week,' Plain-Ann replies.

On the Peach side of Apricot (2)

An article

Years ago I sat on a bus in front of two women who were discussing the colour of the Mother-of-the-Bride outfit one of them had bought the week before.

'What colour is it?'

'Hard to say, orangey.'

'Like a tangerine?'

'Oh no! Not so vivid. When I say orangey, really it's more orangey-pink.'

'Orange blossom, then? That'll be nice for a spring wedding.'

'N.. no, not really. That's *really* pale, isn't it?'

'More of an apricot?'

'Mmm. But pinker.'

'Shrimp?'

'No! Not as pink as that.'

'Coral?'

'No. Not so bright.'

I was hooked; crucially invested in establishing the colour of the frock. 'Peach?' I muttered into the damp air of the bus.

'Peach?' they took my suggestion up.

The Mother of the Bride considered. 'On the peach side of apricot,' she agreed, at last.

I relate this incident because it illustrates a lot about why I am a writer and the writing process. Situations like the one on the bus are meat and drink to a writer. All of life is material to her ever-eager eye and attentive ear. I am a terrible eaves-dropper, as demonstrated above, and I am very nosey; I have a knack of turning a conversation until it's all about the other person 'What have you been up to?' I ask. 'Where have you been? Who have you met?' and then 'Really? Tell me about it. How did you feel?' I ferret story out of the least snippet of overheard chat. I embroider story from encounters briefly glimpsed in the supermarket aisle. For me, they are laced around with narrative potential. What's the back-story? Why is he looking at her like that? Where will this meeting lead? It loops and coils and draws me in, ensnaring me in its possibilities. Before I know it I am inventing dialogue, defining character, conjuring a world of history from the peculiar slouch of a hat over an eye, or a stretched-out silence over a neighbouring restaurant table. The two women on the bus got invested with character. I invented back-story.

Writing is my way of coping with the fragmentary nature of life; we never see *everything*, we never know the whole story. I'll never know where on the colour spectrum that lady's outfit belonged, or how it looked when it was on, or whether (as I rather suspect she did) her neighbour turned up to the evening do in something very similar ('if you'd *said* yours was cantaloupe, I'd never have worn this old thing.'). Life's narrative is always being interrupted by time or diverted by distance; it gets put on hold while the chores are done. The bus carries it away and I never know the up-shot but as a writer I can draw the threads together again, reconnect the severed ends and do away with impediments altogether. Potential becomes actual; I conjure it into being - not only what happened (the beginning, the middle and end), and when, but also why it happened, and how, and who to, and why it matters. I like the wholeness of it, the unity. There's a profound satisfaction in it given by nothing else that I know.

What, amongst other things, excited me about the women on the bus was the whole idea of The Wedding, with all its attendant customs and participant roles. How interesting, I suddenly thought, to describe a wedding from the points of view of the lesser satellites; the Mother of the Bride, the Chief Bridesmaid; the Best Man. There's one for the little book of ideas! I use my writing to test out and explore universal themes and cultural traditions, to question big ideas like family (in Relative Strangers) and consequences (Lost Boys). I use it to tread the roads I have not taken in real life as well as to anatomise in surgical detail every false step and foolhardy choice I ever made. They say that writing is good therapy, and it really is; you can probe the most delicate and profound of issues and often make more sense of them on the page than you can in real life. Of course you can control the outcome, too, unravelling fashion faux pas to knit back into a successful garment. Fiction is a sort of laboratory where you can place something real into an artificial vacuum, test it and stretch it and subject it to unimaginable stresses to see how it behaves. You can vivisect the living flesh or dissect the corpse of regret as long as you bring forth something new and fine - wisdom, understanding, empathy, forgiveness - which will hopefully be of more than simply private benefit. The personal exposure is painful and dangerous but essential; the veracity of real experience beings something vital, I think, to the writer and the reader both.

Sometimes I am asked if my work is autobiographical. I believe that every writer must put something of herself in her work. If she doesn't the reader can tell; it is artificial and doesn't satisfy, like that squirty cream you can buy in aerosols. It looks good for about two minutes but after that you just have a pool of greasy white liquid which is unappetising and doesn't taste of anything. In my writing I strive for truthfulness, to imbue characters and situations with truth which makes them vivid and credible, giving them a life of their own. If things have truth then they have significance - they mean something - both to me and to the reader; we can both vicariously experience, walk in new shoes or see with clarity something that was muddied before.

The effort involved in arriving at this truthfulness - this integrity - is considerable. It is a process of second-guessing: would he really say that, given what has gone before? Would she really do that, under those circumstances? What does a thing *really* look like, smell like, sound like? It has to be right to be real. The efforts of the women on the bus to establish the colour of the frock - the nudging and tweaking, the counter-suggesting, honing and refining - is exactly the process I go through when trying to describe something, to make it vivid and tangible.

Writing is all about connection. I felt connected to the women on the bus, a small cog in the machine of their relationship. Although I never saw either of them again, let alone the apparel in question, the little interaction stayed with me; I had played a part, my muttered suggestion had connected me to them. Our stories had over-lapped, even if only briefly. It is an essential aspect of our humanity, this desire and ability to communicate and connect with one another, to be part of something that is bigger and more important than just 'me'. Much more mysterious than simple physical association, I mean the shared understanding of one person with another, and of the individual with the wider world. Don't we, when we hear a piece of music, or see a beautiful painting, or stare out at night into the star-peppered sky, feel some inner part of us reaching out and becoming part of it? Aren't there moments, with a dear friend or loved one, or, sometimes, even with a stranger, when we know a better peace than we can ever have alone? We experience, just for those moments, a kind of synchronicity; what Mr Spock calls 'mind-meld'. We are told that God is spirit and we are made in his image - as spiritual beings - and it is at these moments, I think, when we ourselves are connected to something other, bigger, better, that we are feeling the spirit most powerfully.

For me, writing is spiritual. When things are going well, I lose myself in it (in reading, also). I have no corporeal awareness while I am writing -

really writing. Hours pass without my having any consciousness of them. I only know what I am reaching out towards something, trying, in the creative process, to touch some truth. Choosing words, dismissing them, choosing better words, sharpening and clarifying, adding texture and hue which will give it - whatever it is - real substance. And then painting in the shadows, the echoes and smells, the antipathies and sudden moods, those resonances which emanate only from that which is true. If this sense of creating, of bringing something out of nothing, isn't spiritual, I don't know what is. I take in what life offers me - offers me, on occasion, in the most unexpected and surprising of ways and on paths which have left my feet cut and bleeding. I garner it into the crucible which is my imagination. What happens there, I don't know - some spark, some mystery I can't explain. The elements rearrange themselves; they coalesce with snippets and fragments I have forgotten about, some metamorphosis happens which is all of me and yet at the same time nothing to do with me. Something entirely new and independent emerges and I set it free in the hope that it will enrich others as it has enriched me.

Thank you for purchasing this book.

Please take a few moments to return to Amazon and give it a star rating. You can write a few words about what you thought.

As an independently published writer I depend heavily on readers' feedback to enhance my profile. I don't have the marketing support of a big publishing house so your opinion really counts.

Please connect with me via my Facebook page and take a look at my website at allie-cresswell.com, liking and sharing and all those good things. I'm on Goodreads, too.

Also by Allie Cresswell

The New Book

A further collection of excerpts, diary entries and new writing.

Contents include: Genesis; Saved; Tea-Drinking in America; Mrs Baggitt's Shop; Being Mandy Broadhead; The Last Passenger; The French Lieutenant's Woman; No-one Was Saved; Moving

In 'Genesis' a writer begins a new work from scratch. It is to be her signature work and the main character will go down as one of literature's greatest. But the character has other ideas about the way the plot should go, and the writer has to decide whether to consign the whole manuscript to the bin or just let the story unfold.

'Being Mandy Broadhead' is a memoire of the writer's teenage years. The agony of being plain and not particularly popular crystallises into a fixation with the prettiest and most popular girl in her school.

'No-One Was Saved' is the outworking of the lyrics of a popular song. Who was Eleanor Rigby and why did she collect rice from the church grounds? What was the face she kept in a jar, and who was it for?

'Moving' includes excerpts from a diary written when the writer moved with her family from suburban Cheshire to rural Cumbria in 2000.

The Hoarder's Widow

Suddenly-widowed Maisie sets out to clear her late husband's collection; wonky furniture and balding rugs, bolts of material for upholstery projects he never got round to, gloomy pictures and outmoded electronics, other people's junk brought home from car boot sales and rescued from the tip. The hoard is endless, stacked into every room in the house, teetering in piles along the landing and forming a scree up the stairs; yellowing newspapers, and obsolete maps, back copies of Reader's Digest going back twenty years, rusted bikes, a rotten greenhouse, moth-eaten clothes... It is all part of Clifford's waste-not way of thinking in which everything, no matter how broken or obscure, can be re-cycled or re-purposed into something useful or, if kept long enough, will one day be valuable. He had believed in his vision as ardently as any mystic in his holy revelation but now, without the clear projection of his vision to light them up for her as what they *would be*, they appear to Maisie more grimly than ever as what they *are*: junk.

As Maisie disassembles his stash she is forced to confront the issues which drove her husband to squirrel away other people's trash; after all, she knows virtually nothing about his life before they met. Finally, in the last bastion of his accumulation, she discovers the key to his hoarding and understands – much too late – the man she married.

Then, with empty rooms in a house which is too big for her, she must ask herself: what next?

Available on Amazon
Readers' Reviews of The Hoarder's Widow

I recommend this book to anyone who enjoys superbly written, character-driven fiction. There is nothing flashy in this simple tale, but it is a rich and filling feast of real and complex characters muddling through life's challenges and finding their way forward together. I would write more, but I need to go find out what else Ms. Cresswell has written, and settle in with a cup of tea and another of her stories.

...a lot of dry English wit, [but] it's certainly not a funny story. Allie Cresswell does a remarkable job of telling of a seemingly ordinary life in a way that you can't put it down. There are twists and turns aplenty, and her lyrically descriptive language paints a compelling picture of the house Maisie lives in.

It strikes just the right balance for me; approachable, allowing me to relax as I read, and elegant, fortifying her scenes and enhancing them with flavours and sensory experiences.

Tiger in a Cage

Who knows what secrets are trapped, like caged tigers, behind our neighbours' doors?
When Molly and Stan move into a new housing development, Molly becomes a one-woman social committee, throwing herself into a frantic round of communal do-gooding and pot-luck suppers.

She is blinded to what goes on behind those respectable facades by her desire to make the neighbourhood, and the neighbours, into all she has dreamed, all she needs them to be. Twenty years later, Molly looks back on the ruin of the Combe Close years, at the waste and destruction wrought by the escaping tigers: adultery, betrayal, tragedy, desertion, death. But now Molly has her own guilty secret, her own pet tiger, and it is all she can do to keep it in its cage.

Available on Amazon and Smashwords or via the author's website at www.allie-cresswell.com

Peer Reviews of Tiger in a Cage

Erudite, character-driven drama at its best. Allie Cresswell is a literary assassin. Just when you think you're safe, the atmosphere and tension in her novels slips home like an undetected, whetted blade between the ribs. What truly makes this novel stand out is the masterful way in which the plot strands are woven together in the final quarter of the book; the explosive events, the straining to release what has been bottled up for decades, the Tiger in a Cage. The climax is satisfying and worthwhile. Highly recommended work from a fine novelist.

Marc Secchia, author of the **Shapeshifter series**.

Cresswell crafts her novels lovingly, taking time to polish them to perfection. She plays with words, linking them together in unique ways, creating stories rich in detail and lavish in language. Her plotlines are subtle and weaving, the characters and their lives all overlapping and inter-connecting in unexpected ways. She is a wordsmith in the true sense of the word.

Ali Isaac, blogger and author of the **Conor Kelly novels**

Cresswell writes about commitment, fidelity, and the gap between public and private lives, as she lays out what we risk when our desires, behaviors, and values are shaped by social convention.

Beth Camp, author of Standing Stones

All of the Combe Close characters are so true-to-life that I am extremely relieved not to be one of Ms. Cresswell's neighbours. I would be terrified of ending up skewered to the page in the next episode...

Deng Zichao, author of People Like Us

Beautifully written with a poetic flow. Allie's love of the English language and ability to generate utterly believable characters is apparent on every page.

Becky Packer, author of the Chroma series

Reader Reviews

'Fun, fluid drama, reminiscent of Austen, but more modern...'

'Cleverly written and intriguing.'

'A deliciously clever read'

Relative Strangers

The McKay family gathers for a week-long holiday at a rambling old house to celebrate the fiftieth wedding anniversary of Robert and Mary. In recent years only funerals and sudden, severe illnesses have been able to draw them together and as they gather in the splendid rooms of Hunting Manor, their differences are soon uncomfortably apparent.

For all their history, their traditions, the connective strands of DNA, they are relative strangers.

There are truths unspoken, but the question emerges: how much truth can a family really stand?

The old, the young, the disaffected and the dispossessed, relatives both estranged and deranged struggle to find a hand-hold amongst the branches of the family tree.

What, they ask themselves, does it really *mean* to be 'family'?

Available on Amazon and Smashwords or via the author's website at www.allie-cresswell.com

Readers' Reviews of Relative Strangers

....makes you think, laugh, and cry

Beautifully written and observed.

...a pleasure to read

a very fine observance of character .... as though she is watching developments from a hidden corner

.....keeps you guessing right up until the end.

I was drawn into the family.

....*the complex politics, desires and heartache of family relationships are at the heart of this book*

a truly compelling read [with] a rich lexicon

Lost Boys

Kenny is AWOL on a protracted binge. Michael is a wanderer on the road to wild and unfrequented places. Teenager Matt is sucked into the murky underworld of a lawless estate. John is a recluse, Skinner is missing, Guy is hiding, Ryan doesn't call.

Then there is little Mikey, swept away by a river in spate.

These are the lost boys and this is their story, told through the lives of the women they leave behind. Mikey's fall into the river sucks them all into the maelstrom of his fate; the waiting women, the boys lost beyond saving and the ones who find their way home.

Lost Boys uses some disturbing, contemporary phenomena; an unprecedented drought, a catastrophic flash-flood, a riot, as well as the much more enduring context of a mother's love for her son, to explore the ripples – and tsunamis – which one person's crisis can send into another's.

Lost Boys was written as four inter-connecting stories along the lines of a palimpsest, where an artist re-uses a canvas in such a way as what is underneath informs and illuminates what is added. The stories are available individually under the titles **Biscuits and Wee, The Other Boy, Stack of One** and **Loose Ends,** or in a single volume, collectively entitled **Lost Boys.**

Available on Amazon and Smashwords or via the author's website at www.allie-cresswell.com

Readers' Reviews of Lost Boys

Lost Boys will have you falling in love with language all over again

A clever interweaving of fate and consequences

....draws upon emotional experiences at many different levels

The joy of the novel is to discover how the characters all have overlapping and intertwining stories

I was utterly wrapped up in the story

Allie Cresswell has the ability to flesh-out all her characters into a reality that kept me totally engrossed right to the last page.

...linguistic banquets of colour, texture, and imagery.

Game Show

It is November 1992 and in the suburbs of a Bosnian town a small family cowers in the basement of their shattered home. Over the next 48 hours Gustav, a 10 year old Bosnian Muslim boy, will watch his neighbours herded like animals through the streets, witness a brutal attack on his sister and be caught up in a bloody massacre perpetrated by soldiers who act with absolute impunity; their actions will have no come-back. The only way he can rationalize events is as 'a game without rules. No-one was in control.'

Meanwhile in a nondescript British town preparations are being made for a cutting-edge TV game Show. It promises contestants dangerous excitement and radical self-discovery in a closed environment where action and consequence bear no relation to each other; the game has no rules, no structure and no-one is in control. 'Game Show' explores issues of personal identity, choices and individual accountability against a backdrop of a war that becomes a game and a game that becomes a war.

Available on Amazon and Smashwords or via the author's website at www.allie-cresswell.com

Readers' Reviews of Game Show

A powerful, disturbing book.

'... Gripping.' 'Compelling.' 'A real page-turner!'

Love this idea and the way the author handles it.

The tension builds up beautifully

All the strands are pulled tighter and tighter together then tied into a very satisfying knot, complete with bow, at the end.

Interview with Allie Cresswell

If you could compare yourself to other, better known writers, who would they be?

I aspire to write literary fiction, with equal emphasis on both those aspects of the genre, so if you tend to read writers who give equal weight to the story they are telling and to the words they choose to tell it, chances are you'll like my books too. Naming names is tricky (how dare I aspire to such august company?) but Ian McEwan, Salley Vickers and Patrick Gale are writers I admire and aspire to emulate. In terms of subject matter, I love the everyday, every-person aspects of Anne Tyler's books. I'd like to think that (with the exception, perhaps, of Game Show) all my stories are the kinds of things which could take place in your neighbourhood to your friends and acquaintances.

What is the greatest joy of writing for you?

The greatest joy is when I sit down in the morning, still wearing my dressing gown and with my first cup of tea still warm in the cup, just to look over what I wrote yesterday, and look up to find it is half past four in the afternoon and the tea has gone cold, with no sense of how time has passed in between but 1800 good words on screen.

Who are your favourite authors?

I love the nineteenth century greats; Trollope, Dickens, Austen, Wharton, James and the Brontes, but unfortunately none of them has produced anything new for some time. The story-telling talent of writers like RF Delderfield, Howard Spring and AJ Cronin was magnificent but sadly they are rarely read these days. Recently I re-read 'How Green is my Valley' and was overwhelmed by the poesy of Richard Llewellyn's prose. I am on the look-out for newer writers. The Reading for Pleasure class which I teach to lifelong learners has really helped. I love Patrick Gale and Alice Munro, Anne Tyler and, Donna Tartt.

What inspires you to get out of bed each day?

Our dogs are always so happy to see me!

When you're not writing, how do you spend your time?

Reading, reading, reading. I believe all writers are readers. It isn't about filching ideas or trying to catch on to the tail of a popular trend, but just about immersing yourself in the world of fiction, walking in other shoes, to broaden your experience and emotional canvas.

I am a member of some Goodreads review groups where I have read some awesomely good (and some cringingly awful) novels. Writing reviews which are honest and constructively critical takes quite a bit of time. Recently two novelist friends have asked me to read their draft manuscripts, which was a great honour.

I have three gorgeous grandchildren and I love to spend time with them, fostering their love of books (but also constructing dens and playing princesses). I like to knit and crochet in the evenings.

Do you remember the first story you ever wrote?

Yes. I was about 8 years old. Our teacher asked us to write about a family occasion and I launched into a detailed, harrowing and entirely fictional account of my grandfather's funeral. I think he died very soon after I was born; certainly I have no memory of him and definitely did not attend his funeral, but I got right into the details, making them up as I went along (I decided he had been a Vicar, which I spelled 'Vice'). My teacher obviously considered this outpouring very good bereavement therapy so she allowed me to continue with the story on several subsequent days, and I got out of maths and PE on a few occasions before I was rumbled.

What are your five favourite books, and why?

Tricky, tricky, tricky. I love nineteenth century literature. Persuasion would have to be on the list along with The Tenant of Wildfell Hall and at least one Trollope: The Last Chronicle of Barsetshire, probably. I was blown away by Donna Tartt's The Secret History. I recently read David Mitchell's Cloud Atlas, which is fab.

Describe your desk

It's a bit of a shambles as I run the house from here, so there are bills and things which need filing, notes to self to remind me about things I'm supposed to be doing, a tangle of wires to charge the 'phone, iPad and Kindle, a cup with cold coffee in it and a pile of books which haven't made it to a shelf yet. I have pens and pencils in a washed out yoghurt pot, and photos of my parents, children and grand-children.
From the window I can see the garden where Tim is building us a kitchen garden with raised beds.

What's the story behind your latest book?

'The Hoarder's Widow' is a development of a story which has been languishing in a drawer for years and years.
We once went to view a house which was packed to the gunnels with every kind of random article you could name; furniture, rugs, mirrors, toys, tools, bikes, bags of rubble, defunct electricals.... We did actually buy that house and the first time we were really able to see it properly was when we got the keys. It had taken the vendors three days to move out - even the rubble had been carefully transported to their new home. Of course I now know that the couple - or, should I say, the gentleman - was a compulsive hoarder. We see a great deal about this on television nowadays. Hoarding is a branch of compulsive obsessive behaviour and is often triggered by a trauma early in life, but is also thought to be a trait which runs in families. My imagination was fired by his wife, the poor, hapless partner of his habit. (I think of her, now, immured in some house surrounded by a further thirty years of his accumulations, probably still having to step over bags of rubble to get to her cooker, assuming the towers of debris haven't collapsed on top of her and trapped her for perpetuity.) I wanted to imagine an alternative destiny for that poor woman, but in doing so I have to come up with a rationale for why she

put up with her husband's hoarding, and an explanation as to what had triggered the hoarding in the first place......

What are you working on next?

I am writing a historical novel, an entirely new departure for me. The story centres on one woman, and spans the 100 years of her life. Once again I have found that a house needs to play a central role. She lives in an ancient pile deep in an un-named but northern county. Somewhere at a distance history unfolds - significant national and international events, popular culture, domestic technology - they all make a belated and somewhat tangential impact on the life of the woman and her house. Getting those details right is proving quite tricky. I had no idea, for instance, that large houses would have had telephones as early as 1920. More important, though, than these advances, are the way experience, relationships and her own moral compass, as well as time itself, impact on the central character and her house.

You have chosen to self-publish your books. Why is that?

Basically because I couldn't get a publisher interested! Of course I'd rather publish in the mainstream. The editorial and marketing assistance I'd get would be invaluable. However publishing, like everything these days, is a business and publishers are looking for big sales figures and film spin-offs. Also, there are a so few publishers and so many writers - thousands and thousands of us - sending manuscripts off to them every week. It would be sheer luck to find my submission on top of an editor's reading pile, then s/he would have to really like it within the first five pages or so. Finally s/he would have to ask; can this be a best seller? Can we make money out of it?
So the chances seemed slim and I took an alternative route.
Indie publishing, unfortunately, because it is totally un-vetted, is full of poorly written novels. You can upload your manuscript in a few moments with only the format checked, not the content, and many people do so

before their book is ready. Readers' reviews are crucial if a book is to rise above the crowd, and will go some distance towards the publicity budget and marketing expertise I'd have at my disposal if I were ever lucky enough to secure a publishing deal, so, if you read one of mine, please return to one of the ebook sites and write a short, honest review.

How can your readers connect with you?

In many different ways! The best way is for readers to respond to my writing by letting me know what they think. A short, honest review on Amazon or Smashwords is easy to up-load.

Visiting my website at www.allie-cresswell.com will allow readers to find a 'Contact me' form, where they can message me with any questions or feed-back. Through that form I can provide some questions to guide reading group discussions about my books, or even arrange to visit to talk about them in person and give a reading.

Finally, of course, there is my Facebook page, where I tend to keep people up to date with the books I am reading, my reviews of other people's books and the process of writing itself.